A WHOLE LLAMA SNOW

KATHY LOVE

ERIN MCCARTHY

ONE

"TEN INCHES? Ten inches of snow. That's a lot." I shot Brandy a dismayed look. "That is not good."

Brandy, my best friend in Friendship Harbor and pub employee, waved a hand in my direction, not the least bit fazed. She returned to filling a wineglass. "This is Maine. That much snow is nothing."

I shook my head, shocked at her lack of concern, then looked back up at the newest addition to my pub, Steamy's decor. A big TV over the bar. And the man, who grinned happily from the screen as if he hadn't just blown all my plans for a romantic getaway right out of the water. Meteorologist Joe Stalling. Or as I liked to think of him, the constant bearer of bad—no, awful—news. Joe Stalling was stalling my love life, and that was not okay.

I was a California girl. Two inches of snow was enough for me to stay inside, curled under a blanket, sipping tea, and pining for sand and sun. I planned to be curled up beside Dean for the weekend, but ten inches on the roads seemed like a lot to navigate.

"They'll have it cleaned up in no time," Dave, my part-time bartender and server, assured me as he leaned a hip on the bar and plucked a maraschino cherry from the metal bar garnish tray. He popped it in his mouth.

"They better. Dean and I have planned this trip for a month."

"The only way we're not going on this trip is if someone dies," Dean said, poking his head out from the stockroom.

I pressed a finger to my lips and shushed him. "Stop! You're going to jinx us."

Given my track record of people dying around me since moving to Friendship Harbor six months earlier after inheriting the pub and house from my grandmother, Sunny, I didn't want to take any chances. Even saying something like that aloud was tempting fate.

"I'm more concerned with the storm delaying the departure of your pals over there," Brandy said, jerking her head toward the table surrounded by my friends visiting from California, still wearing their designer ski apparel. They hadn't even gone skiing today.

Sienna Lawrence, who I had known since I was twelve when we met on the L.A. acting audition circuit, was wearing black Fendi ski pants and mink earmuffs. I knew that because she'd mentioned it three times already.

"Hey, Soph, we're getting super parched over here," Oliver called.

Brandy grumbled something under her breath and noticeably slowed her pouring of the next glass of wine.

I ignored her and nodded to Oliver, managing a smile.

Dave regarded the table of Californians. "It's hard to picture you hanging out with those guys on a regular basis." He studied them as if they were a foreign species as he chewed another cherry. "They don't seem like your kind of crowd."

"Yeah," I said, because I couldn't really disagree. They had all been in my friend circle for years, but after living here, it was becoming harder and harder for me to recall why. Frankly, even Oliver, who I considered my oldest and dearest friend, was starting to get on my nerves. I'd been so looking forward to his visit. Even when he asked if he could bring a few friends, I'd been excited. But it hadn't exactly been the visit I imagined. Now that the show he'd starred in as a kid was being remade, he'd been playing a serious game of one-upmanship with the fellow actors, as they had bragged their way around town, trading pretentious stories. He hadn't really had much time for me.

Brandy plunked the last glass of pinot noir on the tray. "I'll let you bring it over."

I couldn't blame her. I had to admit, I'd probably avoid them too, if they weren't my guests. They were staying in my guesthouse and my main house. "They do tip well," I told her.

That was enough for Brandy to pick up the tray and head over to their table.

"I have to say I'm really disappointed in the skiing here," Brett DiCaprio, no relation to Leonardo, said, loudly enough that everyone in the pub could hear him. "I guess after you've skied the Alps, Maine is one big bunny hill."

"Then I guess you'll probably never come back here," Brandy said, very cheerfully.

Dave snorted.

I winced. This colliding of my two worlds was not enjoyable. Fortunately, they were leaving on a nine p.m. flight that night. If the weather cooperated.

Just then Janelle, another one of my servers, dashed through the door, her coat and old-fashioned stocking cap covered with snow.

"Holy snowballs, it's really starting to come down," she said, brushing off her coat. "The roads are already getting slick."

"Woo-hoo! It's a snowmageddon," Dave cheered.

Oh no. No. Images of the cute bed-and-breakfast in Camden that Dean booked for us flashed through my mind and then faded. I feared much like my chances of actually getting there. I could safely say I wasn't sold on Maine winters. At least not today.

As if reading my mind, Dean caught my hand and squeezed my fingers. I immediately felt myself calm down a little. He had a way of doing that for me. I couldn't count the times he'd reassured me about the finances of the pub—which were still tenuous. But he had a way of making me feel like things would be okay. I squeezed his strong, callused fingers back and gave him an appreciative smile. He smiled lopsidedly, and for a moment, I was dazzled by his dreamy good looks.

But then, that menace Joe Stalling reappeared on the TV, warning more ominous snowfall totals. I couldn't watch anymore, so I stood and wandered over to Janelle. She sat at one of the tables, unlacing her snow-caked boots.

"Janelle, if you want to head home, that's fine. I can't imagine it will be busy today, and the roads are just going to get worse."

She shook her head and pulled a canvas sneaker from one of her coat pockets, then another from the other pocket. She dropped them both on the floor beside her feet, which sported rainbow-striped socks. "We are usually pretty hopping on snow days, and I need to pay for a flamenco class I just signed up for at the rec center."

Flamenco? And here I thought the rec center only offered multiple levels of Jazzercise.

As if to validate Janelle's comment about being busy, the bell over the door jingled and a group of about six or seven snow-covered patrons strolled in, laughing and chattering excitedly.

"I can't believe people want to go out on a day like this," I said.

"Heck yeah, snow storms are fun. Exciting," Janelle said as she tugged off her cap. Her short hair sprung out around her head, making her look like a cheerful baby bird.

I smiled, then walked to the door to peer out. The snow was really coming down. Big fat snowflakes that already covered the steps and walkway. We'd have to keep those cleared if people really planned to come and celebrate snowmageddon here. Snowmageddon. It just sounded miserable.

I sighed and headed over to join the California crowd.

"Hey, Sophie-baby," Oliver greeted me, his hair that was usually dyed any variety of colors now bleached blond and cut short. I wasn't used to seeing him so—well, normal looking.

"Are you done playing pub owner for a bit?" Brett asked.

I tried not to be annoyed. Even when I hung out with this group back in California, I'd never been particularly fond of Brett. He'd played one of Jake's buddies on the show—the gangly, awkward and lovable nerd. Now an adult, he was still gangly and awkward, but he was never particularly likeable, much less lovable. He'd always been loud and obnoxious. Nothing had changed there either.

"I can hang out for a bit," I said.

Oliver patted the empty chair next to him. "I can't believe our vacation is nearly over. I feel like I barely saw you."

I didn't bother to point out that he barely had seen *me*. I sat down.

"This snow is bananas," Madeline said, glancing toward the windows. "I hope this isn't going to mess up our flight." Then she smiled regretfully toward me. "Not that Maine isn't really beautiful, but we're all supposed to be back for a photo shoot for *Entertainment Weekly* the day after tomorrow."

"We have the cover," Oliver added.

The High Jinx of Hayley and Jake was getting a reboot, following in the nostalgic footsteps of *Full House* and *Saved By the Bell*. Madeline had been a part of the original cast, playing the main character Hayley's little sister. Oliver had played the title character, Jake. However, the actress who'd played Hayley, Lori Mariano, had not come back for the reboot. She was the only one of the original teen cast that had gone on to bigger projects. Oliver told me she was currently filming a movie with Adam Driver and Morgan Freeman. I could see why she wasn't interested in reprising the role of Hayley Green. Even if she'd been the plucky idol of a generation. Still, Oliver was thrilled at the opportunity to reprise his role, and I was happy for him. Acting gigs hadn't exactly poured in for him for the past few years.

"We'll be back in time," Rage said, plucking a chip from the seafood nachos in front of him and popping it in his mouth.

Yes, Rage was his name. Just Rage, to no lack of amusement from the pub staff. Rage was brought in to replace Frankie Sarandos, who had originally played Jake's jock bestie. Frankie had declined coming back to the reboot, because he now owned a chain of successful restaurants that kept him busy.

So, the part went to Rage. His looks fit his name. He was bulky and muscular with short-cropped dark hair and intense dark eyes. He reminded me of an MMA fighter, but his physical appearance was where that image ended. I've known him from the auction circuit, too. He was always very sweet and easygoing. And when he smiled, he had two deep dimples that made him look quite charming. He'd certainly been the most pleasant of the bunch during this visit.

Sorry, Oliver.

But it was true. I glanced at my bestie, feeling a little sad that he'd fallen back into the Hollywood pretentiousness. Most of his conversations with me on this visit had been around his extravagant travels and prestigious party invites and lots of name-dropping. Oliver had never been like that, but I suppose the idea of having his lucrative acting career back had gone to his head a bit.

"Yeah, we'll get to the airport, even if we have to hire some hick to take us in their big, old, plow truck," Brett said with his usual smirk. He glanced around the pub. "There has to be a dozen local yokels with a big truck in here right now." He laughed loudly at his own comment.

A couple of the people at the bar frowned in his direction. I didn't blame them.

"Or maybe someone has a horse and sleigh," Madeline suggested. "That would be fun."

"Or maybe we can use Sophie's llama," Sienna added wryly. She stared at me over the rim of her wineglass as she took a long sip.

While Sienna had been a part of our friend group, she hadn't been in the original cast of *Hayley and Jake*. Now, she would play the other lead in the reboot. The producers had opted to just replace the lead without explanation. Like the whole two Darrens on *Bewitched*. Just here you go, viewers, and here's hoping you don't notice. I found the casting a little odd. Sienna was sarcastic and at times just outright a mean girl. The Hayley character had been plucky and an optimistic dreamer. It was going to take some serious acting skills for Sienna to pull that off.

But she was beautiful with dark hair and vivid blue eyes—unfortunately she knew it. She'd batted those eyes more than once at Dean since she'd been here. Not that I was jealous or anything.

Madeline laughed merrily, seeming to miss the sarcasm in Sienna's tone. "We can't all fit on a llama."

Sienna rolled her eyes and took another gulp of her wine.

Rage took Madeline's hand, bringing it to his lips to press a kiss on her knuckles. The two had been a couple for a few months, which made good copy for the reboot. The cast reunites and love is in the air—that sort of thing. Madeline pulled her hand away, but then smiled at the others as she focused on her Cobb salad.

"I'm starving," she said with a slight giggle as she speared a piece of lettuce. Her random giggles and spacey comments never bothered me. She was a ditz, but very sweet. I could see how she and Rage had come together. They both had kind hearts.

"Maybe we should consider leaving earlier," Oliver suggested. "I can set up an Uber for four o'clock."

"That might be a good idea," I agreed readily. I did feel bad for being so eager to see them go, but I wasn't sure I could handle another day with the "almost famous" crowd.

"I definitely have to be back, too," Oliver said. "My agent just got me an audition for a Lifetime movie. *Stalked By My Dentist.*" He'd already mentioned his audition a dozen times over their stay.

Madeline giggled without looking up from poking at her salad.

"I've got to say, it does sound like a winner," Sienna said, then took another sip of her wine. "If you get the part, maybe you can be in the sequels, *Stalked By My Orthodontist* and *Stalked By My Oral Surgeon.*"

Oliver shot her a dirty look. "Jealous much? This could be a breakout role. It's a pretty meaty script."

"It's not a bad gig to be one of the Lifetime sweethearts," Rage said. "You could be the next Eric Roberts. I met him a few times, and he has been very happy with his Lifetime work."

"You met Eric Roberts?" Sienna said, sitting up as if suddenly interested. "I actually met Julia Roberts at a brunch in Calabasas." She leaned back again, smiling smugly.

And here we were again with the one-upping. I lost the battle and rolled my eyes.

"How freaking old is that guy anyway?" Brett grimaced. "I think once an actor gets to a certain age, they should just bow out."

"That doesn't even make any sense," Rage said. "Look at Sir Anthony Hopkins. Or Madame Judy Dench."

"Well, they're British," Brett said as if that defense made any more sense than his original point.

"You're dumb," Sienna said, shaking her head. "You do know at some point you'll be old too, right?"

"I'm just saying," Brett said, not offended as he reached across the table to grab from the nacho plate.

"I could pass that to you," Oliver said, dodging out of the way of Brett's elbow.

"I'm fine," Brett said, oblivious to how rude he was being. I handed Oliver a small plate to give to Brett.

"So, Sophie," Sienna said, sitting up again. "How do you manage to stay in this desolate place? Your acting career couldn't have been that dead."

Sienna was the only one in this circle who had seemed almost gleeful when my own show, *Murder, She Texted*, got canceled. She'd offered me the appropriate condolences, but her bright blue eyes had twinkled when she did so.

"I don't find it desolate," I answered easily. "I actually love it here and I love being a business owner. I'm not thrilled about this snowstorm. But my friends here make up for the weather." Yes, that might have been a bit of a jab.

Sienna looked unimpressed, but added, "I suppose your pub manager does keep it somewhat interesting." She glanced over to the bar, watching Dean as he talked to some of the pub's patrons.

She waved in his direction. He didn't notice. But Dave waved back.

A loud clatter turned everyone's attention back to the table. Madeline leaned down and retrieved the fork she'd just dropped.

"Oh dear, I'm such a butterfingers."

Rage offered her his fork, but she shook her head. "I'm done anyway." She laughed and reached for her wine.

"I'm done too," Sienna announced, shoving her plate of barely eaten clams away from herself. "I don't see how you can eat those things. They are so greasy."

Ogling my boyfriend and insulting my favorite dish that we served at Steamy's. I had hit my saturation point.

"I'll take them," Oliver said, before I could say anything—which was probably for the best, because I was seriously done with Sienna and her bad attitude.

Sienna waved a hand at them. "All yours. They're gross."

Oliver took her plate. I grabbed a clean fork from the setting in front of me and snagged one, popping it in my mouth just to make a point. The fried seafood was crispy and perfect. Clearly, Sienna didn't know a perfectly fried clam from a slug. She was such a flat-lander, as the locals would say.

"I'm going to head back to the guesthouse to pack," Brett said. "Are you going to set up the Uber?"

Oliver nodded, happily chewing. At least, he still enjoyed the food at Steamy's. He picked up his phone in the way of an answer.

"Cool."

I watched as Brett left, going behind the bar and out the back via the kitchen. It was the shortest way to get to the guesthouse, which was in my backyard, but it still struck me as odd how comfortable my guests were with wandering around my business. Then again, I'd known them for years. Maybe Brett considered me more of a friend than I did him.

"Does anyone want another wine?" Madeline asked, waving her empty glass.

"Me," Oliver said.

Rage and I declined.

"What about you, Sienna?" Madeline asked.

"Sure. I basically drank my way through this bust of a week. Why stop now?"

I looked back toward the snow falling past the windows, so the others couldn't see my disgust. All they had done was complain their whole visit. Okay, it was mainly Sienna and Brett, but I'd heard a few grumblings from the others too.

"I don't think this was a total bust," Rage said after Madeline walked away. "Sure, the skiing was a little weak compared to Vail or Telluride, but I still loved seeing Maine and also seeing where you live, Soph."

"Thanks, Rage." I appreciated him saying that.

"Oh, I think Maine is amazing," Oliver said, which made my heart fill with cheer. My friend was back. "It is fun to see a place that seems sort of frozen in time."

Or not.

A group of women came in, dusting the snow off their coats.

"It's a pity the styles seem to be frozen in time too," Sienna said, eyeing a woman with a rather large perm and wide-frame glasses. "The eighties are strong with that one."

"You know," I said, standing. "I really need to get back to work." I was tired of all the jabs, subtle or not so subtle. "The eighties are back in style, anyway. Look at Brett. He's working on a mullet."

Oliver's eyebrows rose at my tone.

The strain of the week and the impending weather had me on edge. I didn't usually let my inner thoughts become my outer thoughts. Whoops. I didn't even feel that bad about it. You don't go to someone's party and tell them the food sucks. Or stay as their guest and complain about every little thing. Sienna needed a lesson in manners 101.

"We need to keep the steps and sidewalk clear," I said as I approached the bar. Both Brandy and Dave looked almost startled by my abrupt announcement. They exchanged a look, then turned back to me.

"I'll keep an eye on it," Dave said, his usual good-natured grin gone and replaced by a somber nod.

I immediately felt bad. I was never bossy and short with my staff. My sharp order was another side effect of dealing with my needy, unappreciative guests, which was not fair. Dave and Brandy —and Dean too—had been putting up with them just as much as I had.

"I'm sorry," I said sincerely. "This whole snowstorm thing has me a little stressed."

Brandy raised an eyebrow. "I don't think that is all that has you stressed. And I can't blame you. Your friends have been pretty crap to you."

I glanced down to the end of the bar, where Madeline waited for her glasses of wine, not wanting her to hear. She had been mostly kind. Plus, I never liked hurting anyone's feelings. She wasn't listening anyway. Instead, she was busy digging around in her purse.

"I expected better from Oliver," Brandy continued.

"I just think he's kind of wrapped up with the reboot of *Hayley and Jake*. I can't blame him for that," I said, trying to give my Cali friend the benefit of the doubt.

"Well, I can," Brandy said flatly.

I appreciated her irritation on my behalf. Brandy hadn't exactly been Oliver's biggest fan before this visit and her opinion hadn't improved.

Brandy poured three glasses of wine.

"I'll bring those to Madeline," Dave said, taking the glasses as soon as she was done.

Brandy shook her head as she watched him rush down the bar toward Madeline. "He has been crushing so hard. Every chance he gets to talk to that chick, he's there."

"Madeline is super cute." Although since she was dating Rage, it didn't seem likely Dave would get much more attention from her than a smile and giggle. As if on cue, I heard her cheerful giggle from the end of the bar.

We watched as Dave placed the glasses in front of her. Then Madeline rose up on her tiptoes and gave him a kiss. A lingering kiss. Brandy and I exchanged looks.

"What was that?" I murmured. Madeline was ditzy, and at times, she could be accidentally flirty because of her capricious nature. But this didn't seem like a thoughtless action. Madeline wasn't so clueless that she had somehow missed Dave's puppy dog adoration all week.

Brandy glanced over at the table where Oliver, Sienna, and Rage still sat. "I don't think Rage saw."

That was good. Not that I could picture Rage reacting as his name might indicate. But it would still be very awkward—and potentially unpleasant.

Dave walked back toward us, a silly, dazed grin on his recently kissed lips.

"You must have a death wish," Brandy said, shaking her head. "What if Rage had seen that?"

Dave shrugged, his bemused smile not budging. "She kissed me."

He wandered down the bar in response to a patron waving for him.

"If he were a cartoon character, he'd be floating right now. Poor sap," Brandy said wryly. She headed into the kitchen.

I frowned, still confused by Madeline's behavior. She was totally smitten with Rage. That had been clear all week. They had doted on each other. Maybe Madeline had simply decided to make the day of her biggest fan in Friendship Harbor. It just didn't seem like something she would do. Madeline was as loyal as she was ditzy.

I glanced back at her. She was back to rooting around in her purse. She looked up and spotted me, watching her. She smiled her usual airy smile and waved. I waved back. Yeah, something was strange here.

"I think I got food poisoning from your greasy, gross pub food."

I turned to see Sienna grimacing at me.

"What?"

"I feel awful," Sienna said. "It had to be those disgusting clams."

I had to admit she did look sick. Her face was pale and her curtain bangs clung to her sweaty forehead.

"I'm sorry," I said, although I was pretty sure it wasn't my food making her feel ill. Oliver and I had also eaten the clams and I felt fine. I glanced at the table. Oliver was talking animatedly to Rage. He looked just fine too. "I think I have some Pepto upstairs. I can get it for you."

She shook her head. "I'm just going to go lie down until it's time to go."

"Here's your wine," Madeline said, appearing beside us. She held the glass out to Sienna.

The beautiful brunette swallowed and turned chalky white. For a moment, I thought we were headed to a full-on Exorcist moment. But she swallowed again, then managed to say, "I don't want it now." More sweat glistened on her brow and cheeks.

"Are you okay?" Madeline said, her brown eyes growing wide with concern. I took the wine from her hand, which she still had jutted practically in Sienna's face, and I set it on the bar. Far away from Sienna. Madeline shot me an "oopsy" look, then seemed to remember she still held another glass. She took a sip.

"I'm going back to the guesthouse," Sienna said. She started down the bar toward the kitchen, using the same route Brett had. Although this time, I couldn't exactly resent her for taking the fastest route. She looked really bad.

"Do you want me to go with you?" Madeline called after her, but Sienna shook her head without looking back. She kept going, picking up speed. When she shoved open the swinging, kitchen door, she practically barged into Brandy, who held a full tray of food on one hand.

"Hey," Brandy cried, as the tray tilted dangerously, but she managed to regain control before food and plates clattered to the floor. Sienna didn't even acknowledge her, racing past her.

"I hope she's going to be alright," Madeline said, gaping after her.

"Me too," I said, sharing a look with Brandy. Sienna would have been more than sick if she had actually knocked that tray of food out of Brandy's hands.

"I hope she is going to be okay to fly," Madeline added.

I glanced toward the windows. The snow was really coming down. Between the snow and Sienna being sick, I had a sinking feeling the likelihood of anyone getting out of here tonight was looking pretty bad.

TWO

MY MUSCLES BURNED and my arms shook as I managed to awkwardly half toss/half drop another shovel full of snow to the side of the pub steps. I'm pretty sure I also made an agonizing groan as I did so, but I couldn't be sure over the pain and the pounding of my heart in my ears. I'd never again claim that my Pilates class was a killer workout. I stopped, leaning heavily on the handle of the shovel. My breath billowed out of my mouth in rapid misty clouds. This was exhausting. And I'd only managed to clear the steps to the pub. I surveyed the sidewalk in front of me. The pile of snow there looked as daunting as Mt Everest.

I seriously considered crying, but the tears would just freeze to my face and I'd be even more miserable. Tears were supposed to be cathartic, not potentially cause frostbite.

"What are you doing?" I heard a familiar voice behind me.

I was too exhausted to even bother to turn and look at Dean. "We have to keep the steps and sidewalk cleared," I said through deep breaths.

Dean tramped down the steps, taking the shovel from my gloved hands. I wasn't quite ready to lose the support, so I sank down on the step, ignoring the cold snow on my butt.

"I was going to do this. I just wanted to get the walkway to the guesthouse cleared."

"I wondered where you disappeared to," I said, the words still jerky through my ragged breathing. I needed to add some serious cardio along with my Pilates.

"I didn't want there to be any reason your friends couldn't get back to the guesthouse and pack their things," he said with a smirk.

I lightly punched his leg, but I couldn't disagree with his reasoning.

"You should have asked Dave to do this," he said, giving me a concerned look. I could only imagine how bad I looked, caked in snow and on the brink of collapse.

"I didn't want him to lose out on his tips. Plus, I'm a strong, independent woman. I can shovel snow." Who was I kidding? I was strong and independent, but I never wanted to shovel snow again in my life.

"You are absolutely those things. But you also look like you're freezing."

"I'm actually sweating and freezing at the same time. Is that even possible?"

He laughed, his deep, delicious chuckle warming my insides, even as I was pretty sure my rear end was frozen to the step. I used the step to brace myself to stand, but it was Dean's strong hand that helped pull me to my feet.

"Go inside and get something hot to drink," he said, his voice gentle and deep, having the same effect on me as his laugh.

I nodded, suddenly too tired to pretend I wanted to be anything but taken care of.

I looked behind me at the steps I'd just shoveled. They were already layered again with more snow.

"Do you really think they will be able to get to the airport?"

Dean looked around. The sky was an oddly bright white as if the sun was trying to reassure me it was still up there somewhere above the storm. But the relentless fall of snow blurred the buildings across the street. It wasn't quite a whiteout, but it was getting there.

"I think the plows will get to these roads soon. I'm sure they are taking care of the major routes first. But yeah, I think they'll make it."

I appreciated his reassurance, but he didn't sound like he believed it any more than I did. He started shoveling.

"I could find another shovel and help you." My offer sounded even less convincing than his plow prediction had.

He smiled, both of us knowing my offer had been only out of politeness. "Nah, go in and get warm." He leaned forward and gave me a quick kiss. His lips were cold, but still warmed me.

"When you get a chance, you might want to go check on the new dishwasher," he added. "The last time I saw him, he was on the back steps talking on the phone and dishes were piled everywhere."

I groaned. We had a dishwasher curse. Either they quit after a day or two or they never showed up to begin with. And now this one showed up but didn't work. Great. I'd be the first to admit, it wasn't a fun job. I knew, because I'd had to fill in several times over the last few months. That's why I decided to increase the hourly pay, even though we didn't have much money to spare. And I definitely wasn't paying more for the new guy to be chatting on his phone in the snow.

"I'll go check on him. And I'll also tell Oliver he might want to make sure his Uber is still on schedule."

Dean paused, holding the shovel mounded with snow, midair. I marveled that his arms didn't even shake, which was pretty darn attractive. I never thought I'd ever find a man shoveling snow swoon-worthy. My, how my life had changed. "That's a good idea. Oh, and could you also check with Dave to see if he remembered to fill the generator. I asked him to check it a few weeks ago, but I forgot to follow up."

"We have a generator?"

"Not a great one, but decent enough to keep the pub going for a couple hours if necessary."

That was good to know. I should probably also know where it actually was and how it worked. I started up the steps, my legs already stiff from the workout and the cold, when the pub door opened. Oliver popped out without his coat, immediately cringing at the freezing temperature and the snow.

"Hey, I was wondering where you were," he said. "Wow, you look like the Abominable Snowman."

"I feel like it too." I had snow everywhere. And I really regretted sitting down on the step. My butt was freezing—and damp. "I was trying to clear the steps. Until Dean saved me."

Oliver grimaced again, but then looked past me to Dean, turning on his full smile. "Dean, the hero. You are always the gentleman."

Dean chuckled. "That's me, alright." He started shoveling again.

"Is everything okay?" I asked Oliver.

He nodded. "I just wanted to let you know I'm going up to your place to pack. We've decided we should head to the airport as soon as we can."

I glanced back at the street. The snow was not lessening. In fact, it seemed to be coming down harder, if that was possible.

"Yeah, I was going to suggest that, too. Dean said the plows should be coming through soon." I didn't add that Dean had sounded less than certain about that.

He nodded and started to head inside, but stopped to call out to Dean. "I'd totally get my coat and come help you, but I really need to pack."

Dean stopped, not hiding his amused disbelief. Yeah, Oliver's sincerity was even weaker than mine had been.

"No worries, Oliver. I've got it," Dean said, returning to his work.

Oliver followed me inside the pub. I shrugged off my parka,

clumps of snow falling all around my feet and causing puddles on the worn hardwood floor.

"My whole body is frozen," I muttered, trying to run my fingers through my wet and icy hair.

"It's bad out there." Oliver stood, still looking out the window of the door. "Although Dean does make it a bit more pleasurable. He looks all manly out there. I bet he's nothing but solid muscle."

"I'm not discussing his body with you."

Oliver gave me a questioning look. I ignored him. He spent half his time teasing me about my new boyfriend and the other half being far too curious about my new boyfriend.

"Come on," he prodded. "Throw me a scrap here. You know I've been single forever."

"You were dating someone last month."

Oliver closed his eyes and groaned dramatically. "That's sooo long ago."

I laughed, feeling a glimmer of my usual connection with him.

"Alright." He sighed. "If you are going to be no fun at all and not share any yummy details about your hunky boo, then I guess I really should get packing."

"I'll come up in a minute." Despite our less than stellar visit, I was sad to see him go. "I have to check in with Dave about the generator we apparently have here. And then I have to tell my current dishwasher to get to work."

"Generators and dishwashers. It's a glamorous life you lead, my friend."

I smirked at him. "It's not that bad." In fact, I didn't mind it most of the time. Well, aside from shoveling and having to take over dishwashing duty, which meant I didn't intend to come down too hard on the dishwasher. I suppose a lazy dishwasher was still better than no dishwasher.

"Okay, I'm going up. See you after you whip your staff into shape." He headed to the stockroom that connected to the pub office and to the stairs that led up to my part of the house.

"Hey," Brandy said as I approached the bar. "I just got a text from my silver fox." She grinned excitedly.

Brandy's silver fox was an FBI agent, who'd been here in December to investigate a mob hit that happened to take place in my guesthouse. Needless to say, I hadn't mentioned that creepy detail to my guests. Oliver knew, which was part of why he'd been staying in my place. Thankfully, he hadn't told them either. I could only imagine what Brett and Sienna would have to say. If they thought the skiing was bad, they'd really flip out about staying in the guesthouse of doom.

Brandy came around the bar and held out her phone to me. I took it and read their very brief text exchange. Brandy had texted first, telling him we were having a big snowstorm and asking how things were where he was. He answered saying they were getting hit, too, and it was a good time to stay inside, stay warm, and stay safe.

"That's nice," I said, handing her phone back to her. I smiled, not sure what she expected my reaction to be.

She looked down at her phone, rereading the short messages again. "Don't you think it's sweet how concerned he is about me?"

This was probably a good time to mention that when Brandy referred to the FBI agent as "her" silver fox, that was completely from her perspective alone. She had spent the last two months analyzing and reanalyzing every text she got from Special Agent Mark Winters. And every one of them was no more personal than this one. They certainly weren't laden with intimate innuendos and devotions of love. But Brandy had taken finding hidden, romantic meaning in his straightforward replies to a truly awe-inspiring level.

"I think he just meant he wants you to be safe," I said carefully. I knew my pragmatic assessment wasn't the one she wanted to hear. But seriously, I'd gotten more romantic texts from Oliver.

To my relief, she nodded, not taking offense. She studied her phone again. "But that's really thoughtful, right? I mean, to take time to send me a text to be sure I'm safe." She looked at me clearly seeking confirmation.

And here we went again—diving headfirst down her hidden-romantic-meaning rabbithole.

I was pretty sure I'd told random strangers to be safe with more emotion, but I wasn't going to tell her that. Nor was I going to mention that his text hadn't exactly been unprompted. She had texted him first.

"I'm sure he does care that you're safe." I always tried to stay noncommittal to her leaps in reasoning. I didn't feel it was fair to build her hopes up too much. After all, they hadn't even spoken to each other outside of texts since he'd been here. But totally destroying her carefully built fantasy seemed cruel too.

She nodded again, smiling wistfully. "He really is such an amazing man."

"Well, you need to remember you are an amazing woman." See, I was getting good at this noncommittal thing. Plus, it was true. Brandy was totally amazing. A single mom, a hard worker, smart and funny and beautiful. She didn't need to waste her time waiting for texts from a guy hundreds of miles away, who I suspected didn't even think about her until her next text message popped up on his cell phone screen. She needed a guy right here in Friendship Harbor, who was genuinely crazy about her. Really, I should be trying harder to help her find that guy.

But right now, I had to reprimand a work-shy dishwasher.

"Have you seen Henry?"

That got Brandy's attention away from analyzing the three-sentence text. She made a disgusted face. "That guy is a creep. He's been hanging around outside most of the afternoon. Talking on his cell and pacing. He's seriously off. I actually think this one is the worst."

That was saying a lot, because she had dated one of the past dishwashers who turned out to be married with four kids. He ended up ghosting us all. I had spent two weeks picking up dishwashing duty because of him. I hated to think this new guy could be worse.

Taking a deep breath, because I really didn't like this aspect of the job, I headed into the kitchen. To my pleasant surprise, Henry was at the dishwasher, spraying down dishes and placing them in the rack to be run through the machine. Jimmy, my cook, was at the grill, frying hamburger patties. He didn't even look up as I entered the kitchen. Typical for Jimmy.

I stood there for a moment, debating if I should still say anything to Henry. It seemed sort of after the fact now that he was back to work. Apparently, I was as good at rationalizing as Brandy was. But I really did hate confrontation. Maybe Henry was just having a bad day or a family emergency or something. Oh yes, I could rationalize with the best of them.

I settled for asking, "How's everything going in here?"

Jimmy nodded, not looking up from his burgers. Henry eyed me, his gaze wandering over me. Then he smiled, showing a glimpse of yellowed, overlapping, front teeth. "All good, boss."

I managed a slight smile back. "Good. We are keeping an eye on the weather and will let you leave if things get worse. But right now, the pub is actually quite busy."

"No problem, boss. I don't live far anyway." Henry grinned again. Something about his smile made my skin crawl. And it wasn't exactly reassuring to know he lived nearby.

Jimmy nodded and flipped one of the burgers.

I started to leave the kitchen, when the back door flew open and Brett burst into the room, his suitcase and ski bag banging on the doorframe as he wrestled with them to get inside.

"What are you doing?" I said more sharply than I intended, but the creepy vibe of the new dishwasher and the sudden dramatic entrance had me on edge.

Brett didn't seem to notice. "I texted Oliver, and he said to bring all our stuff over here. The Uber is supposed to pick us up in front of the pub."

That made sense. I moved to help him with his suitcase, so he could use both hands to get the long ski bag through the door, rather than breaking his skis, or more importantly, my doorframe.

"How is Sienna?" I asked once he was inside.

He frowned. "I don't know. I haven't seen her."

"Really? She went back to the guesthouse a while ago. She wasn't feeling well."

"Oh, I did hear someone come in, but when I called out, no one answered." He shrugged. "The bathroom door was closed when I left to come over here. She could have been in there. Speaking of which, I need to go to the john, too."

He headed to the swinging door out to the pub, nearly hitting me with his skis. I ducked and grabbed his suitcase again. "Let me help before you break something."

He willingly let me take it. The hardside suitcase weighed a ton, even though it had wheels.

"I can help," Henry said, appearing close to me, his body practically touching mine. He smelled oddly musty and I could feel his hot breath on my cheek. I quickly released the handle and backed away.

"That would be great, Henry," I managed. I noticed Jimmy had turned from his grill and was watching us. But as usual, I couldn't read the older man's frizzled and wrinkled expression. Still, his presence helped calm my tension. Jimmy might be a man of few words, but I knew he was a good man. I had my doubts about Henry—and Brett, for that matter.

I waited as both men struggled to get the luggage out into the pub. Brett dropped his ski bag to the ground, blocking the space to get behind the bar and rushed toward the men's restroom.

Dave immediately came and picked the bag up. "When you gotta go, you gotta go, I guess."

Henry laughed, his chuckle oddly high-pitched and eerie.

Both Dave and I stared at him.

"Thanks, Henry," I said, just wanting away from him. "I'll have Dave help me from here. And we do need those dishes washed."

He eyed me for a moment, then nodded. "I'm on it, boss."

"Dude," Dave said after he'd disappeared back through the swinging doors. "That guy ain't right."

I didn't say anything, but it was safe to say, I'd be putting up another ad on Indeed for a dishwasher. At this rate, I might as well leave the ad up.

"Let's just put this stuff over there." I pointed to the corner closest to the pub door.

After we were done, I started to go check on Madeline and Rage where they still sat at the table. They should be packing, too. I paused a few feet from the table. From their body language, I could tell they were quietly arguing about something. Rage tried to reach for Madeline's hand, but she jerked it away and took a large gulp of her wine.

As long as I'd known her, Madeline had never been much of a drinker. She'd told me back when we were in our late teens or early twenties that she never wanted to fall into the trap of so many child actors. So, she'd always been more of a kale juice and clean living type than a party girl, but she'd had more than a couple glasses of wine today. Of course, she wasn't a kid anymore, and she could certainly do whatever she wanted. But it seemed unusual.

I started to walk away, not wanting to intrude on whatever was going on between them, but before even making a step, Madeline called out to me. "Sophie!"

I turned back. She waved me over, her movement broad and overexaggerated. She was definitely tipsy.

Reluctantly, I joined them.

"Have a seat," Madeline said, gesturing to the empty chairs like Vanna White selling a vowel.

I looked at Rage, waiting for him to indicate it was okay with him, too. He nodded, but I could tell from his drawn expression that I had been right when I thought they were fighting.

"Were you about to go pack?" I said, giving Rage a way out if he wanted it. "I know the others are getting their stuff together."

"I guess we should. Mads, you stay and visit with Sophie. I can go get our stuff," Rage said, starting to stand.

"No!" Madeline cried, startling us both. Then she giggled, looking back and forth between our shocked expressions. "No. I'll go too. That's too much stuff to carry by yourself."

"I don't know—" Rage started, clearly concerned about Madeline's drunken state.

"I'm going," she said, pressing her hands on the table to stand. As she did, she hit a full glass of wine, sending a wave of red liquid across the table. "Oh no."

Brandy saw or heard the accident and rushed over with rags from the bar. We both began mopping up the mess.

"I'm sorry," Madeline said, far more stricken than the spill merited. "I'm so sorry." Her face crumpled and she started to cry.

I stopped wiping up the mess, moving to hug her. "It's not a big deal, Madeline." She turned onto me, burrowing her face against my shoulder. I shot a worried look at Rage, who was also now standing on the other side of her. He looked dismayed, too.

"There is never any reason to cry over spilled wine," I said, rubbing her shaking back.

"If we did that, we'd be crying every day," Brandy added as she still cleaned up the mess.

Madeline lifted her head, her big brown eyes still teary, but she managed her cute, albeit watery, giggle. "Well, I guess it was actually for the best."

I smiled. She was right. She'd clearly had enough to drink already.

"Come on, babe," Rage said gently. "Let's just go get our stuff."

She nodded and he slipped his arm around her back, leading her toward the kitchen.

Brandy let out a low whistle. "She's good and toasty."

I nodded. "It's weird, because I've never seen her that way."

"Well, I did overhear them fighting. I didn't really catch what it was all about, but she didn't look happy."

I considered that. "Probably just a lovers quarrel."

"Maybe Rage saw her kiss Dave." Brandy piled the wet rags on the plate of Madeline's barely touched salad and headed toward the kitchen.

I went to the bar and grabbed a clean rag and a tray and returned to the table to finish clearing it. I placed the toppled wineglass on the tray, then the one Rage had been nursing since lunch and finally the one Madeline had been drinking when I had first approached the table. The two of them had half-filled glasses—and a full one? Wow, Madeline was double-fisting. She really must be upset about something.

"Hey," Brett said, approaching the table. "Where did everyone go?"

I picked up the tray. "Everyone's packing."

"Well, they better get moving. Oliver said the Uber would be here in an hour and that was a half an hour ago."

"I'm sure they will all be ready." I headed to the bar. Brett followed.

As if on cue, Oliver appeared with his bags. "You never made it up. Generators and dishwashers take some time, huh?"

Oh no, I hadn't gotten around to asking Dave about the generator. Of course, things had been a little crazy. I'd get to him soon. Right now, I had to see my friends off.

"All the others are still getting packed," Brett said, clearly irritated.

"Well, I'm going to have a drink," Oliver said, not worried.

"That is one perk of staying at a guesthouse behind a pub. Plenty of booze." Brett settled onto a barstool. Oliver sat on the one beside him.

Dave took their orders, while I headed to the kitchen to drop off the tray of dirty glasses. Jimmy was working on filling three bowls with fish chowder, while Brandy waited. They were the only ones in the room.

"Where's Henry?" I asked.

"Two guesses," Brandy said, annoyed.

"Seriously, he's on his phone again?"

Brandy nodded and I thought I heard Jimmy mutter something that sounded like "worthless," but I wasn't sure.

The back door opened, and I expected it to be Henry returning. But it was Rage and Madeline with their luggage.

"That was quick," I said. Both of them looked calmer—and Madeline even looked like she was a little less tipsy. The freezing weather had a sobering effect.

"We were already packed," Rage said.

"How is Sienna? Is she going to be okay to fly?"

Madeline frowned, then looked at Rage and then back to me. "We didn't see her. There wasn't anyone in the guest house."

Okay, that was weird.

"Maybe she went to your house to find Oliver," Rage suggested.

"No," I said. "I don't think so. Oliver is all packed and sitting at the bar with Brett."

"Well, she must be around here somewhere," Rage said.

The door opened again, and we all turned expectantly toward it. Even Jimmy.

Henry stepped in, coming to a stop as he saw us all staring at him.

"Hey," he said slowly. "I was—umm, just taking a small break."

"Again," Jimmy muttered from behind us. He slammed the lid on his chowder pot to accent his irritation.

Brandy placed the three bowls of chowder on a tray and exited back into the pub. I didn't blame her for getting the heck out of there.

"You haven't seen our other friend out there, have you? The brunette woman," Rage asked. From his stance and the set of his jaw, I could tell he didn't get any better feeling from Henry than I did.

Henry shook his head. "Nope, I only saw you two walking across the yard to come in here."

"We didn't see you," Madeline said. She looked nervous.

"I was around the side of the house."

I frowned. Did that mean he was near my part of the building? The rest of the staff respected that while the pub was part of my house, the two spaces were kept separate. I didn't like the idea of this guy just wandering around my property.

"Well, let's go see if she's waiting with Oliver and Brett," Madeline said. She tugged on Rage's arm.

Rage glared at Henry for a moment longer, then let Madeline lead him away.

Henry walked farther into the kitchen, watching them leave. "I guess those Hollywood types are pretty dramatic, aren't they?"

I shot him a disapproving look, then followed my friends. As soon as I stepped into the pub, I could see the others were gathered at the bar, but no Sienna.

"I haven't seen her since she left the table, saying she wasn't feeling well," Oliver was telling the others as I reached them.

"Well, she's got to be around here somewhere," Rage said.

"Maybe she went to the airport without us," Madeline suggested.

Brett shook his head. "I saw her skis and other stuff in the guesthouse. I don't think she'd leave without her stuff. I mean she probably didn't want to carry it herself, but she wouldn't just leave it."

"Did anyone try to call or text her?" I asked.

Oliver pulled out his phone and unlocked the screen. He tapped and scrolled, then held the phone to his ear. Everyone watched.

After a moment, he shook his head and hung up. "Her phone is ringing, but she didn't answer and it went to voicemail. I'll try texting her."

This made no sense. She couldn't just disappear. "I'm going to go check the guesthouse," I said.

"I'll go with you," Oliver said. His cell phone chimed. "Wait, maybe this is her."

We all watched him again. He opened his text messages. "Oh great."

"Is it her?" Madeline asked, looking nervous. "Is she okay?"

Oliver shook his head and sighed. "It's a text from the airline. Our flight has been canceled."

Brett swore and ran a hand through his curly hair. "Well, that just sucks."

I couldn't agree more.

Behind the bar, the television volume grew louder. Brandy held the remote, and she and Dave stood staring up at the screen. We all joined them.

The prophet of doom, Joe Stalling, stood in front of the weather screen, pointing to a swirling blob over a good portion of Maine. "Now, this was one of the outcomes that I mentioned could be a possibility for us previously, and it looks as if that is what is happening. Due to high pressure in the north and a slowing of the jet stream, the storm has stalled over a major portion of the state. That means the snow totals are going to be much higher than I had initially predicted. In some areas, we will be looking at totals of up to three feet. There will be whiteout conditions, high winds and a lot of drifting snow. If you don't need to be on the roads, then absolutely don't. We are looking at a wild nor'easter out there."

A gust of wind whistled around the windows as if to punctuate the forecast.

"Wow," the female newscaster said with appropriate enthusiasm. "It does look like we are in for a wild ride."

Several of the patrons started to gather their things, obviously taking the report seriously.

"Well, this is freaking awesome," Rage muttered.

"I think we should still try to get an Uber," Madeline said, her voice panicked.

"Why?" Brett said. "The flight is canceled."

Madeline grabbed Rage's arm and hugged it to her. "Please, Rage. I'd rather get to the airport and get a hotel room there. That way we can already be there to get the next flight out."

"Even if we could get an Uber, which I doubt, what about Sienna?" Oliver pointed out reasonably. "We can't just leave her."

"I'll go look in the guesthouse," Brett said.

"I'll go with you," I said, going to get my coat. "I need to check on Jack, too."

"Do you want me to go with you, too?" Oliver asked.

"No," I said, shrugging on my already damp parka. I leaned into him and whispered, "Try to convince Rage and Madeline to stay here." Madeline was still holding Rage's arm, pleading with him to go. Clearly, the wine still had her not thinking straight. "It's insane to try to leave now."

Oliver nodded. "I don't think they could get an Uber anyway, but I'll try to get her calmed down."

I followed Brett into the kitchen. Both Jimmy and Henry were there.

"It sounds like the weather is supposed to get really bad. You guys should probably just head home." I didn't wait for either of their responses, following Brett out into the blowing snow.

"It's freezing," Brett said, his words sounding oddly distant in the wind. I nodded, tugging the hood of my parka tight around my face. It was so cold. Snow pelted my face and I lifted my shoulders as much as I could to protect myself.

Between the new snowfall and the drifts, Dean's hard work shoveling a path to the guesthouse was almost gone, but we followed what we could of the faint trail. Each step was like walking in quicksand, my boots sinking into inches of snow. Brett slipped, but managed to catch himself. I thought he swore, but I couldn't quite hear him through my hood and over the wind.

We made it to the guesthouse, tumbling through the door, breathing hard and shivering. After shaking off the snow and getting our bearings, we looked around.

"Sienna," I called. The house was silent except for the whistling of the wind.

Brett trudged through the living room and down the hallway. "Her suitcase is still in her room."

I walked to where he stood in the bedroom doorway. I rose up on my toes to see over his shoulder. The suitcase was open on the floor. "It doesn't even look like she finished packing."

Brett turned, and practically bumped me over. I caught his arm to steady myself. He grimaced at me, then his frown morphed into a lecherous grin "Why, Soph, are you moving in for a little Brett-action?"

I dropped my hand from his coat and backed away in disgust. "Gross, Brett. Get a life." I didn't wait for his response, moving to check the bathroom. The door was still closed. I knocked. There was no response. "Sienna." I waited a moment longer, then eased the door open. The room was empty, but I saw some makeup and other toiletries on the sink. She definitely hadn't packed.

I checked the bedroom at the end of the hall. It was empty.

"She's not here." And I didn't feel good about it. Where was she? The wind howled again. "You can head back and see if she's there. Or maybe she called Oliver back."

"Where are you going?"

He clearly hadn't heard me when I'd said back in the pub that I needed to check on Jack.

"I'm heading to the barn to check on my llama."

Brett made a face. "It's just an animal. I'm sure it's fine."

Just an animal. Obviously, he didn't understand how special Jack was to me. "Just go back. I'll be in as soon as I make sure Jack is okay."

"Whatever."

Brett left.

"Thank god," I muttered, glad to see him go. Between his icky comment about Brett-action and not caring about my beloved pet, he was falling even lower in my esteem. Not that he had much lower to go.

I hesitated, then went back to Sienna's room. Her clothes were only half packed. I debated, then wandered in, going through the clothes scattered on the unmade bed. There was nothing unusual. I went to her suitcase. More clothes. All designer brands, I noticed. I wondered how she could afford such expensive things. She hadn't been acting much herself. Of course, they all looked new, so maybe she'd gone on a recent spending spree, banking on the *Hayley and Jack* reboot to be a big success.

I unzipped the inside pocket on the suitcase flap. Some lotion and lip balm slid out. I pulled the pocket open wider and peeked inside. There was a lighter. And a sunglass case. And something that looked like a pen. I reached for it, realizing it wasn't actually a pen. It was a vaping device.

I wasn't overly surprised. Sienna had smoked occasionally when we were back in California. I dropped it back inside, then reached in again. I pulled out a few colorful rubber tubes. What were these? I let one dangle in front of me. It was a tube about ten or so inches long and made of latex. I took a neon pink one and stuffed it in my coat pocket. I wasn't even totally sure why. I shoved all the contents back in the pocket and zipped it, then started to leave only to pause in the hallway.

Instead of heading for the door, I headed to the bathroom. Sienna's toiletry bag still sat on the counter. With one finger, I pulled it open. Somehow doing that made it seem less like I was snooping. The case was filled with expensive makeup, from Shiseido face cream to Loubilaque Lip Lacquer. Those two items alone cost as much as all my makeup put together. I poked at the items, spotting something underneath her makeup. I looked closer. It looked like a syringe. I quickly pulled my hand out of the bag and backed away.

Sienna had done a stint in rehab in her late teens. It hadn't been a secret. In fact, the tabloids had a field day with yet another child star falling into the same trap as so many others. Sienna had been totally humiliated by all the bad publicity. She hadn't wanted to be another statistic, and she definitely hadn't wanted to be another TMZ or Access Hollywood story. I think that more than anything made her stay clean. And as far as I knew, she had done a good job staying away from anything but alcohol--although she'd been using that pretty liberally during her stay here--so it wasn't out of the realm of possibility that she could have gotten back into other things.

Suddenly, I just wanted to be out of there. I pulled my hood up and braced myself to head back out into the storm. The snow pelted me as soon as I stepped outside. I pulled my hood tighter around my face and hunched forward to block as much of it as I could. The snow had to be a foot deep already. I trudge toward the barn, recalling a movie I'd seen where a farmer or rancher had to tie a rope from his porch to the barn to use as a guide so he didn't get lost when going to care for the animals during a blizzard. I wondered if I should have done that myself. Not that I had any rope that long. Or that I could really get that lost. I did live in the middle of town. Even if I was blinded by snow, I'd stumble onto a house at some point.

Way to be melodramatic, Sophie.

I struggled through the snow, glancing up to see the barn and fence not far ahead. Argh, this was awful. Once I reached the barn, I might just curl up with Jack and stay there. It wasn't as if I wanted to head back to the pub and listen to my friends whine and complain about being trapped here. Somehow, this would probably be my fault, even though I had mentioned several times over the past couple days that they were predicting a storm.

I looked up again to gauge my distance to the barn. So close. Hallelujah.

Then my foot caught on something, and I snow-plowed face-first into a drift of snow. I cursed. Not usually my style, but this was seriously miserable. I rolled over from my belly and onto my back. More snow fell in my face, blinding me. I cursed again and pushed myself up to a sitting position. I wiped my face, which given my gloves were caked in snow too, didn't really help. But after a few more swipes I could sort of see. I pulled in a deep breath and placed my hand beside me to struggle my way back onto my feet. Then I froze. Sticking out of the snow next to me was a foot. A foot clad in a mink-lined boot.

I screamed, the sound getting lost in the howl of the wind.

THREE

MADELINE JUMPED up as soon as Dean, Brett, and Rage trudged back into the pub. "Is it Sienna?"

Aside from their builds, it would be almost impossible to tell them apart because of their layers of winter clothes and covering of snow. Rage peeled back his scarf to reveal his pale, drawn face. His expression alone was enough of an answer, although I already knew I'd found our missing friend.

I joined Madeline, waving my hands for all of them to keep their conversation quiet. I didn't want any of the few remaining patrons to overhear us.

"Yes," Dean answered quietly, when it became clear that Rage was in shock.

"She's dead," Brett added. "Frozen stiff." His voice was a little louder than I would have liked, but I was more rattled by the callousness of his words to shush him.

Madeline burst into tears. I immediately rubbed her back, shooting Brett a disapproving look. Brandy offered her a handful of drink napkins.

"What?" Brett said, having the nerve to look offended. "I'm just answering her question."

Madeline sobbed louder. Seriously, was Brett that clueless-- and classless? We were talking about a friend of ours. Sienna might have been rude and self-absorbed at times, but she deserved some respect. She certainly didn't deserve to be dead in a snowbank.

"I know it's hard, Brett," Oliver angrily whispered, "but try to have a little tact."

Brett's look shifted around to each of us, confused. "Okay, fine. Go ahead and shoot the messenger." He stormed away to shuck off his snowy outerwear.

Oliver and I exchanged looks over Madeline's shuddering frame.

Rage finally registered his girlfriend's distress. He stripped off his coat and hat and dropped them on one of the barstools as he came over to her. Oliver and I backed away, letting him take over.

"It's okay," he said, pulling her into a hug. "It's okay." He didn't sound like he really believed his words, but they still seemed to work. Madeline calmed a little.

With Rage taking over the job of comforting her, I went to Dean. "Are you alright?"

This was the second time in as many months that he'd seen a dead body. I'd offered to go out with Rage and Brett to see if it was Sienna, but Dean hadn't let me. Probably my dramatic, stumbling, screeching entry into the pub after tripping over her had given him the valid impression that I wouldn't handle officially identifying her body very well. He was right. But I still hated that he felt like he had to do it.

He shrugged out of his coat and said quietly, "Yeah, I'm okay. She isn't frozen stiff. But she's definitely dead. I couldn't really tell how long she was out there. She was completely covered in snow, but it's drifting so much, it's hard to tell anything."

I looked toward the windows at the front of the pub. I couldn't see anything but heavy, blowing snow. It was getting darker, too.

Behind me, I heard Brett call out for a shot of whiskey. Great, all we needed was for Brett to be obnoxious *and* drunk.

"Should we call Justin? Can he even get here?" I pulled my cell phone out of my pocket anyway.

"Yeah, we should let him know. And maybe find out if we should move the body or not."

I frowned at Dean. "You don't think it's just an accident?"

"It probably is, but we should still talk to the sheriff."

He was right. I tapped my phone, scrolling to Justin's number. It was pretty sad that the local sheriff's number was so high up on my recent calls list.

The phone rang several times before Justin finally answered. "Sophie, is everything okay there?" I could tell by the noise on the other end of the line, he was outside. He was talking loudly, but his voice still sounded distant.

"No one had an accident or anything?" he prompted when I didn't answer right away. "It's a crazy night, and we have a lot of people off the road and trees down. Can whatever you are calling about wait?"

Of course, the police were swamped on a night like this, and it wasn't as if anything could be done for Sienna now. And she wasn't exactly going anywhere. But I still thought we needed him to come, when and if he could. "Umm, well, it's kind of important. My friend, Sienna, who was visiting from California, is outside."

There was silence on the other end of the line other than the sound of wind.

"Justin?"

"Okay, is she lost or something?"

"She's dead."

There was another pause, then he said with weary acceptance. "Of course, she is."

"I'm sorry," I said, both for adding to his already stressful night and for the fact this wasn't exactly an unusual situation for me. I was starting to feel like maybe my grandmother had left me a house and pub built on a cursed Native American burial ground or something.

"I'll be there when I can," he said, some of his words muffled by the howl of the wind around him.

"Okay. Be safe out there." I wasn't sure he heard me, before the line went dead. I hope that wasn't a bad sign. I sighed, staring at the screen for a moment. "He said he'll be here as soon as possible."

Dean nodded. He looked like he was going to say something, but Oliver's raised voice drew our attention toward the bar.

"That's complete BS." Oliver rose from his stool and glared at Brett. Oliver wasn't normally one to be aggressive. He preferred snark to showdown. But from the furious look on his face and the way his hands were fisted at his side, I wasn't sure he was going to stick to his usual creed. "Why would you even say something like that?"

I hurried to the bar, frowning. "What is going on? And can we discuss it quietly? I don't want the patrons involved in this."

I didn't mean to invalid anyone's feelings about all of this, but it was still a business--and well, I had that rather pesky track record of dead people around me. That was just the sort of thing that could really hurt a business. Bad food, bad service, potential of death in the owner's general vicinity—the usual stuff Yelp reviews complained about.

Oliver glanced at me only to return his enraged stare at Brett. But he did lower his voice. "Our friend here is just being his usual charming self. Sienna is lying out there in the cold and snow, and he's claiming that she OD'd."

Brett lifted his hands and gave us all an innocent look. "What? It makes sense, right? How else would she just die like that?"

"You know what? You are really messed up." Oliver sat back down on his barstool, but turned his back to him. He took a large gulp of his wine.

Brett shot us another confused look. "I'm not trying to be a jerk, but it seems like the only reasonable explanation to me."

Madeline whispered, "You think Sienna was into drugs?" She didn't wait for anybody to answer before adding, "I mean it makes sense. I kind of thought she had been acting weird since we got here."

"Weird how?" I asked, remembering the rubber tube in my pocket and the thing that looked like a syringe back in the guesthouse.

Madeline looked almost surprised that I had asked. She shrugged. "I don't know. Just strange."

That wasn't exactly a helpful explanation.

Oliver shot us an incredulous look. "This is ridiculous. We all know Sienna has been clean since her teens."

"How do we really know that though?" Madeline said. "I mean when was the last time we all really hung out. I bet I hadn't seen her for over a year until we found out we'd all been asked back for *Hayley and Jack*."

"I don't want to think that she would fall back into something hardcore, but it does make sense," Rage agreed.

Oliver shook his head. "Well, I don't buy it. I talked to her pretty regularly over the years, and I never got the feeling that she was doing anything. Plus, she was really excited about the reboot. Why would she mess up this opportunity?"

That was a valid point, too. But if she was back into drugs, that meant she wasn't thinking clearly. I couldn't say that I'd noticed anything during our interactions this week that would lead me to believe she was high. But the truth, I had kind of been trying to avoid them for much of their trip. So, I wasn't sure I was the best person to make a judgment on that. But whatever the cause, we needed to know what happened. And I did find those suspicious items. But I wasn't going to mention that now. I didn't want to upset Oliver even more.

"I contacted our local sheriff. He will be here soon." I hoped. And I'd tell Justin what I found. "We need to stay put and see what he can find out."

"A sheriff?" Madeline gaped at me. "Do we really need to do all that?"

I knew Madeline could be a bit of a dingbat, but she had to know we couldn't exactly have someone mysteriously die in a snowbank and not follow up with some sort of emergency services.

Brett turned on his barstool. "Yeah, that is kind of overkill, isn't it?" He paused. "Overkill. That was probably a bad choice of words, wasn't it?"

"You know what?" Oliver announced, shoving off his stool. "I need a break from you all." But he only looked at Brett. "Let me know when my old buddy the sheriff arrives." He strode into the stockroom and into the office, presumably going up to my place. I debated following him, but I suspected he genuinely wanted to be alone. He had been the closest to Sienna in this group. He probably needed a little time to process all this.

"Nice one," Brandy said dryly to Brett from behind the bar.

Brett shot her a dirty look. "Great. Now the locals are turning on me."

"I'm not sure there was very far for me to turn," Brandy said before disappearing into the kitchen. Brett scowled at the swinging kitchen door.

"Having the police come is just standard procedure," Dean explained.

Madeline turned to Rage. "I think we should just go. Call an Uber and we can just stay at a hotel near the airport. That way we can be sure to get on the next flight back to L.A."

"Mads, we're not going to be able to get any car service tonight," Rage said reasonably. "You've seen how bad it is out there."

She grabbed the sleeve of his thermal t-shirt, her wide eyes frantic. "Please. I don't want to stay here." Her voice rose an octave in her panic. "How are we supposed to stay here with Sienna out there?"

Rage put an arm around her and pulled her close. "I know it's really unpleasant, but we're fine here, and we'll make it to the airport as soon as the snow lets up."

Madeline looked as if she wanted to argue further, but instead she nodded and allowed Rage to lead her to a table by the window.

Once she was settled, he went to the bar and ordered her a glass of wine. I wasn't particularly sure that she needed more wine. But this was all very disturbing, so who was I to judge how any of them got through it? Except Brett. If he drank and got more obnoxious, I was totally going to judge him.

"Do you think we should tell the staff to head home?" I asked Dean. "I know it's already really bad out there, but it's just going to get worse."

"I actually think it would be more dangerous for them to leave at this point," Dean said. "Plus, they should all probably stick around until Justin gets here. I know they weren't involved in Sienna's death, but Justin might want to know if they saw or heard anything."

That was true. "It's just so weird that she died out there. I mean she couldn't have been out there long enough to actually get hypothermia, could she?"

Dean shook his head. "It seems pretty unlikely to me. I think the drug theory is more feasible."

"I did find some odd things in the guest house," I said, keeping my voice low, so none of the others could hear. I told him about the items. "And she looked really sick when she left here to go back to the guesthouse."

Dean considered that. "Like withdrawals or something?"

I shrugged. I'd never gotten into the drug scene in L.A. In fact, more than that I'd avoided that type of thing totally. "I think I'll do a roll call just to see exactly who was here and where they were during the time Sienna was gone. It seems like someone would have to know or have at least noticed something."

Dean gave me a knowing look. He totally had my number when it came to my curious nature. Well, I like to call it curious, but I knew Dean would probably call it nosy. And maybe a little suspicious. But to be fair, so far, I'd had good reason.

"In *Murder, She Texted*, my character solved a case simply by making a list with the times and locations of all the suspects."

He raised a hand. "I saw that episode."

I smiled, partly because I was secretly thrilled that he'd actually seen every episode of my short-lived TV series, all on his own without me even forcing him, and partly because I knew he didn't actually want to be a part of my crime-solving plan.

"Not the best episode," he added.

Some of my warm fuzzies faded. He smiled, letting me know he was teasing. "It doesn't seem like there is really anything suspicious about this. Drugs. Maybe even a heart attack or aneurysm. Things like that do happen."

"I agree. It probably was something like that," I said, even as my Spidey-senses tingled a little. "But it's good to be prepared, you know, just in case. Plus, it will be a help to Justin. He sounded pretty stressed when I called. Really, I'm just trying to make things easier on him."

He gave me an indulgent smile. "You just can't resist, can you?"

"What? He said he was really busy tonight with the storm." I tried to look innocent. "You know I'm a helper."

He gave me a look. "Is that what we are calling it now?" He zipped up his coat. "Well, I'm going to leave you to your list and head back out to shovel the steps again."

I frowned. I hated that he had to keep doing such hard work. "Is there really any point right now? It's still a mess out there."

"Well, we should try to keep them clear. If it piles up too high, we'll never get it clean. We'll need a path, especially with Justin coming. And if he can get the EMTs here, they're going to need access, too."

That was a good point. I thought of Sienna still out there. Yes, we did need a way to get her body to the coroner's.

"Plus, I don't want to interfere with your sleuthing," he added, his eyes twinkling.

"I'm not sleuthing. I'm helping."

He gave me one last disbelieving look, then headed to the pub door. Snow blew in when he opened it. He quickly stepped out into the swirling sea of white. I had to admit I was glad he was going out there and not me.

Now for my list. Not of suspects, I reminded myself. Just people who might have noticed something. I searched around by the cash register for a piece of paper. I settled on a server's pad.

The pub had emptied out. Most of the patrons had the good sense to get home and settled in for the night. Only a few stragglers remained.

Not unexpectedly, George Sprague, one of our regulars, sat at the end of the bar with his usual beer and his usual John Deere hat perched on his head. I wandered down to the bar to him. "George, what are you still doing here? Shouldn't you be home with your wife and kids?"

He gave me a look as if I was crazy. "Go home and be stuck with the old lady and all my wild kids? Heck no, I'll take being snowed in here any day over that."

I laughed, although I was pretty sure he wasn't joking. George spent more time here or at work than he ever seemed to spend with his family. He seemed like a good guy, at least from what I saw, but it did make me wonder what kind of relationship he had with his wife that he would rather sit at the end of our bar and nurse a beer all evening. And his parenting obligations weren't much of a priority either.

"Seriously, George, I'm afraid you're going to get stuck here if you stay too much longer."

He took a sip of his beer and adjusted his cap. "Oh, I'll be alright. My wife and kids are actually in Lewiston visiting her mother, so I'll probably stay for one more and then just walk home."

Well, it made me feel good that he wasn't just avoiding his family. Though sometimes I wondered if his wife had left him years ago and he just hadn't noticed it yet. But I still didn't like the idea of him walking home. Not in this weather. Outside the wind whistled and rattled the pub windows. But I could also understand not wanting to be by myself tonight either. It was an eerie, desolate night. Of course, Sienna's death didn't help that feeling.

I raised the server's pad in front of me and wrote down his name. "So, George, I don't suppose you saw or heard anything going on with my friends this evening?"

"Plenty. Your friends are a different sort, aren't they?"

I couldn't really deny his assessment. I also wasn't sure I wanted to go into everything he potentially heard. "They can be. But did you hear anything specifically about Sienna?"

"Like what?"

"Oh, I don't know." To be honest, I had no idea what type of information I was looking for. If Sienna had died due to natural causes, or even a drug overdose, what exactly was I expecting to find out? It wasn't as if she was going to shoot up in the middle of the pub. I just decided to stick with the facts for George himself.

"You were just sitting here all evening, weren't you?"

George adjusted his hat again. "Are you thinking there's something unusual about the death of that friend of yours?"

"No, not really."

"Well, since you moved to this town, things have been a little weird. So, could be, right?"

I shot him a slightly offended look over the top of my pad. Although, how could I really disagree with him?

"Thanks, George," I said, making a note that he'd been at the bar the whole night. "Can I get you a new beer?"

He nodded, then leaned forward over the bar. "I did hear one interesting thing about that gal."

I looked up from my note-taking.

He casually tilted his head toward the table where Madeline and Rage sat. "I did overhear those two arguing about the girl who died. It sounded to me like the guy had been caught in a sticky situation with the dead girl, and the cute redhead was none too happy about it."

"Really?" I glanced at my friends.

Rage had been in a sticky situation with Sienna? How sticky?

From what I had seen of him and Madeline this week, they'd seemed nothing but head over heels for each other. I wouldn't have thought Sienna could even catch Rage's eyes long enough to get him into a "sticky situation." But, and I hated to speak ill of the dead—or rather think ill of the dead—but Sienna had always had an unfortunate, and unattractive, habit of being interested in other women's men. I'd always tried to see it as some insecurity she had in herself, rather than a true malicious streak. But since she'd made more than one flirtatious comment to Dean over the past week, I'd been struggling with that excuse. I made a note of George's observation on my pad. "Thanks, George. Let me get that beer for you."

He nodded.

I headed down the bar to where Brandy stood, watching evil Joe Stalling. "Any new updates?"

Brandy sighed. "They are saying over three feet. This is the worst nor'easter we've had in years. And just in time for your very first winter here."

"Lucky me. Hey, can you get another beer for George?"

"Sure. I guess he's going to be here for the night, huh?"

"I wouldn't doubt it. He's in no rush to leave, that's for sure."

"I think we're all in for the night." Brandy grabbed a pint glass and went to George's usual brew.

"You can head out, you know. I know you need to get home to Ethan." She really should be home with her son. I should have sent her home hours ago, frankly.

Brandy shook her head, topping off the glass. "He's with my mom. I don't think I could get home now anyway. The tires on my old car aren't exactly what you'd consider snow-ready. Heck, they are barely road-ready."

That was true. I'd been in her car many times. Her car was just one step away from being sent to the wrecking yard.

"Well, you can stay with me," I offered.

She grinned. "I was planning on it."

She headed down the bar, and I added her name to the list, but I didn't bother to make any notes next to her name. Brandy had been here working all day. Not to mention, my Maine friend had tried to have as little to do with my Cali friends as possible. I added Dave, too. He had also been behind the bar all night.

I considered what George had just told me about Rage and Madeline and Sienna. Suddenly, Madeline kissing Dave made more sense. Although I felt a little irritated that Madeline had been using Dave to make Rage jealous. Dave was a sweetheart, and he didn't deserve to be dragged into some jealous game. I didn't like that.

I added Jimmy, also with no notes. Truth be told, the older man probably hadn't even paid a bit of attention to my friends, even though they had been barging in and out of his kitchen all week. I also wrote down Henry, the leering dishwasher. I put a question mark beside his name.

I jotted down all the names of my California friends, making notes. Oliver had been in the pub most of the day, but he was upstairs for at least part of the time that Sienna was gone. I couldn't imagine him ever doing something to Sienna. He had liked her and it just wasn't his nature. Oliver killing somebody was almost laughable, frankly. You know, if murder was funny. This was a guy who had to leave the room when we were watching *The Wizard of Oz*, because the flying monkeys were too scary. We'd been twenty-one at the time.

Of course, any thoughts of murder were all speculation anyway. I added Madeline and Rage, circling my note about them possibly having a fight with Sienna. Although, they had been in the pub all day. They did leave to get their luggage, but they'd only been gone a very short time.

Brett, however, had gone to the guesthouse for quite a while. He said he hadn't seen Sienna, but who knew for sure. I noted that.

I looked around the pub. A couple I knew from their frequent visits rose from their table, bundling up to leave. I considered asking them to stay until Justin got here. But if he decided he needed to talk to them, they were local and I'm sure he knew where they lived. I noticed that they had snowshoes, leaning against the wall beside their table. Clearly, they couldn't live far away if they were snowshoeing home. And how very Maine of them.

Then I spotted another couple, who I hadn't noticed nor did I recognize tucked into the far corner of the pub. I studied them. It was pretty rare for me to not at least recognize my patrons. Pad in hand, I wandered to their table.

"Hi, folks," I greeted.

The couple were in their mid-thirties and they both sat on one side of the table, close together, facing out toward the rest of the pub. Despite their close seating arrangement, I didn't get the vibe they were huddled together because this was a romantic lunch or something. I noticed right away that they weren't dressed in the usual bulky sweaters or sweatshirts and jeans that most of the locals favored on cold days. The man wore a tailored, button-down shirt and wool trousers. They looked expensive and professional. The woman also wore a tailored shirt and pants. Neither of them wore boots. Definitely not Mainers.

"How are you this evening? Is there anything else I can get you?" I could see the remnants of our burger platters and a couple of empty pints. "Another beer maybe? Or dessert?"

The man looked up from his phone, grimacing at me as if I was interrupting something important. Another sign this wasn't some romantic outing. Unless, he was just a really jerky boyfriend. He looked like he could be a jerky boyfriend.

The woman smiled politely, if not exactly warmly. "No, I think we are all set. We will just take the check."

She dismissed me by picking up her own cell phone that sat on the table beside her. I watched them for a moment, until the man noticed my presence and cocked an impatient look at me. I went back to the bar.

"Hey, Brandy, have you been waiting on that couple in the corner?"

Brandy glanced in their direction. "Yeah, I have been." I could tell by her less than enthusiastic tone that she hadn't gotten a better feeling from them. "They are friggin' rude. Why?"

"I was just curious if you got any feel for who they are. Are they from town?"

Brandy shook her head. "No, I commented on the fact they seemed pretty busy. They've been on their cell phones constantly. And at one point, the woman was on a laptop. They said they were from out of town and here for business. Although I have no idea what business that would be. Friendship Harbor is a fishing and tourist town. It's not like we have any Fortune 500 companies here. And those two scream both urban and money to me."

I had to agree. "Okay, that is weird."

"They've actually been here all day. And they are talking in these hushed tones, but when I'd go up to check on them, they would stop talking altogether."

They could just be socially awkward, but yeah, they definitely seemed odd.

Brandy, regarding them from down the length of the bar, asked, "Do you think they are up to something?" She shot me an eager look.

I think it was safe to say that Brandy loved a mystery even more than I did.

"I don't know. But right off the bat, I got a strange feeling about them."

Brandy nodded, her eyes glittering. "You know, I did too. I feel like when they weren't on their phones, they were just watching everyone. It's a little creepy."

That was creepy—if it was true. Brandy could get a little exuberant in her search for clues or suspicious people. But they did seem out of place. That much was certain.

"Do you mind if I bring them their bill?" I wanted to see if I could find out a little more.

Brandy shrugged, although I didn't miss her look of disappointment. She handed me the check billfold from the front pocket of her apron. "Get their story. I'm super curious."

I nodded, then headed back to their table.

"Here you go. Are you sure there's nothing else I can get you? We have an amazing brownie sundae. And homemade blueberry pie. We use locally raised berries."

"We're all set, thanks." He pulled out his wallet and held up a credit card to me without even looking at the check.

I took it, but didn't move away from the table. "I hope you don't have far to go tonight."

The man scowled at me, but the woman smiled. It looked forced and didn't quite reach her eyes, but it was still better than Mister Grumpy-face.

"We're actually just down at the waterfront."

"At the Friendship Harbor Inn?"

She nodded.

"So you are from away, then," I said cheerfully, using a Maine-ism, to make myself seem more authentic. Locals rarely said "from out of town" They said "away" as if anywhere outside of Friendship Harbor was some vague location in the universe. Not that I got the feeling these two would actually warm up to some local charm, but it was worth a shot.

"Yes." That was all she offered.

"Where are you from?" I knew that was being pushy, but I smiled widely and tried to play it off like I was being just an overly friendly local.

"If you don't mind," the man said abruptly, "we're trying to get something done before we leave this establishment."

Well, alright. I tried not to be offended by the judgy way he said "establishment."

"No problem." I waved his card. "I'll be right back." I hurried to the bar, not looking at his name until I was at the cash register. "Bryce Holden."

Why did that name sound familiar?

I pulled the pad from the back pocket of my jeans and wrote the name down. Behind me, I heard the pub door open, the howling wind growing louder and a gust of frigid air reaching me all the way from across the room.

Dean and Justin walked in, quickly closing the door behind them.

"I'll finish up cashing out this check," Brandy said, appearing beside me. "Go deal with the sheriff and your friend."

I nodded, suddenly worried what Justin would discover when he went out back to take a look at Sienna.

FOUR

THIS WAS MISERABLE. On so many levels.

I shielded my face deeper in my hood and tugged up my scarf, but the snow still pelted my upper cheeks and forehead, and the wind burned my skin. I wanted to flee back to warmth, but I felt like I needed to be out there with Justin and Dean. Sienna had been my friend, after all.

Rage had joined us too, although I didn't really know how to feel about him being there given what I had learned from George about a possible tryst of some sort between Rage and Sienna. I supposed right now, I should just be thankful for the added help.

The three men were on their knees, digging the snow away from the body with their hands. So far, I could see Sienna's legs, poking out of the drifted snow, reminding me of the Wicked Witch of the East after the house landed on her.

"I don't think we can do much more tonight than get her out of the snow. There is no way emergency services can get here. Maybe we can put her in the shed?" Justin yelled over the wind.

I couldn't hear Dean's reply, but I stepped closer, my movements awkward as my foot sank into the snow up to my knee. I wasn't thrilled that Sienna would have to remain on my property, but Justin was right. The storm was raging too hard.

"I have some blankets in Jack's barn," I shouted. "I can get one for you to put Sienna on. That might make it easier to carry her."

I didn't wait for their answer, struggling through the snow to get to Jack's paddock. By the time I got there, I was out of breath and my lungs burned from the workout and the freezing air. I leaned against the fence, gathering my strength to fight with the gate. Fortunately, the snow had drifted away from the fence, and after several hard shoves, I got it open enough to squeeze through.

One thing was for certain, if I ever inherited property in Alaska or the Antarctic, I was going to take a hard pass. This was so not my scene. I made it to the barn, again thankful that the small over-hang shielded the door enough that I could slide it open. When I fed Jack this morning, I'd had the forethought to leave the lights on. I didn't want my fuzzy friend hanging out in a gloomy barn all day. I could hear Jack moving and snuffling in his stall.

"Hey, Jack," I called out to my beloved pet. I heard more move-ment and then a white fluffy head appeared over the top of the stall door. He pitched his big banana ears forward. That was his way of letting me know he wasn't exactly happy. He didn't like being cooped up alone all day in his stall, and I couldn't blame him.

"I'm sorry, buddy." He made a low purring sound, which was a good sign. It appeared I was forgiven. I walked over and scratched his head and ears. Then gave him a kiss on his cold snout.

"Oh, you are cold, too. But don't worry, you'll be warm soon enough." I planned to bring him inside my house. There was no way I could leave him out here with a dead person. That just seemed like terrible pet ownership. And especially not with Sienna. She'd never been an animal person. I gave him one more quick kiss on the nose and then grabbed a wool blanket from a pile against the wall.

"Okay, Jack, hang tough. I'll be back soon."

He rumbled deep in his furry chest, which generally meant he wasn't totally pleased. I swear he actually understood what I was saying to him. "I'll be right back. Honest."

I tugged my hood and coat around myself, half tempted to

wrap the blanket around me, too. Bracing myself for the onslaught of wind and snow, I headed back out into the cold. By the time I stumbled and waded through the deep snow, the guys had finished uncovering Sienna's body. She looked surprisingly peaceful, her dark lashes against her cheeks and her frozen hair, wavy and spread out around her. Her skin had a strange, bluish cast and clinging snow made her shimmer in the lights from the pub and the guesthouse. If I didn't know the truth, I could imagine her made up for the part of a winter queen, oddly lovely and ethereal. If she had to die this young and in such bizarre circumstances, I know she would actually be pleased that she looked so beautiful in death. And it had been in a rather dramatic fashion--she'd have liked that, too.

I handed the blanket to Dean, and he and Justin spread the gray wool out on the snow as best as they could with the whipping wind.

"Okay," Justin shouted, gesturing to me and Dean, "if you two can take her feet, we can get her arms." He pointed to Rage, but Rage didn't appear to hear. He just stood, motionlessly staring down at Sienna.

"Rage," I called. He still didn't respond.

"Rage," Dean yelled louder.

Rage startled, physically jolting. "Yeah," he said, and even through the gusts of wind, I could hear the daze quality in his voice. It was hard to see Sienna this way. But I couldn't help wondering if he was so shaken for a different reason than just seeing a friend dead.

"Help me with her arms," Justin repeated, and this time Rage moved to help lift Sienna onto the blanket. Our movements were awkward, although that was primarily due to the deepness of the snow rather than the weight of Sienna.

"Okay, everyone take a corner," Justin directed and we began to slowly half-carry/half-drag her toward the shed. Getting her through the gate was a bit of a struggle and at one point she got wedged, but fortunately Rage and Dean were strong enough to lift the blanket and squeeze her through, while Justin balanced her. At this point, I had lost all my strength and mainly followed along behind them trying not to topple over in the high snow. Once we were inside, the guys settled her on the far side of the barn.

We watched as Justin did a cursory check at the body. "I don't see any signs of trauma, but I will have the coroner here to pick her up as soon as I can. Hopefully later tomorrow."

I headed over to Jack, who had poked his head out over the top of the stall to watch. His ears were pitched forward again, and I wondered if the animal realized Sienna was deceased. Animals did know these types of things, and my llama was particularly clever.

I grabbed his harness and opened the stall to put it on him. He willingly stuck his nose into the straps as if he was as ready to be out of this barn as I was.

"Are you planning to bring him inside?" Dean asked. He hadn't been overly thrilled with having my pet in the pub when I'd done it once before, but I definitely was not leaving Jack behind.

"Well, I can't leave him here," I said reasonably. "Not with…" I stopped as Rage sent me an incredulous look.

"You're worried about your farm animal. But we're just going to leave Sienna out here like this."

It did seem heartless of me, but Jack was very much alive and Sienna was well…

Okay, I did feel awful about Sienna being left out here, and I didn't know what to say, especially when I could see how torn up Rage was. I knew we all were. But with the storm, what other choice did we have? And I wasn't going to lie, I didn't want a dead body in my house. Or the guesthouse. As it was, the guesthouse had already seen it's fair share of death. The place was probably already haunted.

Fortunately, Justin came to my rescue. "I know this seems really harsh, but honestly, this is probably the best place for her. The cold could preserve some evidence and make it easier for the coroner to do his job."

I didn't know if that was actually true, but I was willing to believe it. At any rate, we couldn't have a body thawing out inside the pub.

Rage remained beside Sienna's body, looking down at her. Then to my surprise, he crouched down and arranged her arms slightly crossed over her body. Carefully, he pulled the blanket around her as if tucking her into bed. The gentle gesture was heartbreaking, but also almost loving, again making me wonder how involved the two of them had actually been.

"Okay," he said, standing up and heading to the door without looking back as if he couldn't bear to be in here any longer. I grabbed Jack's lead and we all headed back to the pub.

By this time we reached the kitchen door, all of us were caked in snow. Big chunks of ice clung to Jack's wooly fur. The animal made a noise that I'd never heard as soon as we all loaded into the warm kitchen. A sort of low keening noise through his nose. I took the sound to be the equivalent of a sigh of relief. I totally got it.

I pushed down my hood, letting out a low noise of my own. My skin smarted from the sudden warmth, but the pain was worth it to be back inside.

Jimmy glanced up from chopping onions, only raising an eyebrow slightly at the sight of several frozen humans and a large llama in his kitchen. He went back to chopping. As was expected, Henry was nowhere to be seen, although I hadn't noticed him outside either. But then again, I had been focused on one goal and one goal only. Getting out of the tundra.

"Sorry, Jimmy," I said through chattering teeth. Even though this was my pub, the kitchen was definitely Jimmy's domain. He might not have said anything, but I was pretty sure having an animal in his kitchen was not something he was thrilled about. Especially not a two-hundred-and-something-pound llama. Nevermind the health codes I was definitely breaking right now. I tugged on Jack's leash and he ambled along behind me into the pub proper.

"Oh yeah," Janelle said happily from where she leaned on the bar eating a cup of chowder. "Our mascot is back. Mr. Steamy Jack himself. The coolest llama in Friendship Harbor."

I appreciated her enthusiasm. I always appreciated anyone who adored my pet as much as I did.

"Well, he's only making a brief appearance this time," I said.

I had kept him in the stockroom the previous time he'd been here, and although he did pretty well with his time in pub lock-down--only shredding a couple rolls of paper towels and helping himself to some dried pasta--I figured I should find a better place for him to stay this time.

The office was out, too many cords and wires that he might try to nibble on. And frankly, we couldn't afford to replace our computers right now if he decided to chew on anything. Jack also wasn't keen on stairs, so getting him up to my place wasn't going to happen. The best solution was to let him hang out in the hallway at the bottom of the stairs leading to my part of the house. The area was big enough that he'd have space to move around and room to sleep. And well, if there were any potty accidents on the floor, I could mop it up with no problem.

Beside me, I heard the muffled ring of a cell phone. Justin pulled the ringing device out of the pocket of his brown sheriff's jacket, checked the screen, then answered, "Sheriff Pelletier speaking." He wandered away from us to speak more privately.

"I'm going to put Jack in the downstairs hallway," I said to Dean, who I noticed didn't even have the good grace to disguise his relief. "I know, I know, you have a thing about animals in the pub."

"I think most people do," he pointed out.

"Well, they clearly don't appreciate what an amazing creature he is. I mean look at this face." I gestured to Jack's handsome mug. "Those majestic ears. That nose. And his eyes. Look at those lashes."

Dean wasn't swayed. Really, I was just messing with him, since I knew he wasn't as much of a fan of my pet as I was. Dean and Jack had a bit of a love/hate relationship. And I really did get

Dean's concern. Pack animals in pubs were generally frowned upon.

"Do you need any help?" he asked, not so subtly nudging me to get Jack out of there.

I sniffed with feigned indignation. "No, Jack and I can handle it."

"Aww, I think he should stay," Janelle said, setting down her chowder cup and coming to scratch Jack's neck. "He's just so cunning. Aren't you, Jackie-boy?"

It had taken me a while of living in Friendship Harbor to realize the word cunning was not used the same way in Maine as it was in the rest of the world. In Maine, for whatever unknown reason, cunning meant adorable. And I couldn't agree more, but I did need to get him out of here. But not before I scruffed the other side of his neck, and cooed, "That he is."

Jack made his pleased purring noise and Dean rolled his eyes skyward.

I sighed. "But grumpy Dean is right. Large animals in a pub are kind of a no-no."

Janelle clearly wasn't ready to stop making her case for Jack to remain here. "It's a snow day. There are no rules on snow days. I say we let him stay."

Dean frowned at the server. "Please, please, do not encourage her."

Janelle shot him a sassy smile, but then sighed. "Party pooper. I think he's a good addition here."

She gave Jack a quick kiss on the snout, then went back to her chowder. Janelle was more than a little eccentric, so I suspect she would think a large llama was a good addition just about anywhere. Most people would not agree.

Fortunately, everyone but my friends and the staff—and George Sprague—were gone. Then I noticed the couple who had seemed so anxious to leave were still seated in the corner. They both watched us, and the man had his cell phone raised in our direction. Was he taking pictures? He seemed like the kind of jerk who would show them to the health department. Great.

Dean noticed them, too.

"Don't worry," I said, quickly prompting Jack to follow me. "He's leaving right now."

I led him into the stockroom and through the office. He did try to stop to inspect a wire that ran across the gray carpeted floor to our printer, which further confirmed the hallway was the best spot for him.

"Okay, buddy. Here's your home sweet home for the night." The wind whistled around the door that opened out to my house's front porch. "Or maybe longer."

Jack rumbled as if to let me know he wasn't totally sure about his new digs.

"It will be fine," I assured him. "Once I get you some blankets and food." I groaned.

Darn it, I had forgotten to bring in some of his food from the barn.

"Okay, let me get some towels to dry you off. And let me warm up for a minute and then I'll go get you some food." I made a face, already dreading the thought of going back out into the storm of the century. Of course, it wasn't just the storm that had me feeling apprehensive to go back out there. I would have to see Sienna again.

I pushed the thought aside and dropped his lead to go up the stairs. Jack wandered over to the hooks near the front door, where several coats hung. He snuffled them.

"I'll be right back. Do *not* chew on anything." I wasn't sure that I could actually get that kind of promise out of a llama, but it seemed like the thing to say.

I doubled my steps up to my house. When I opened the door into my kitchen, I found Oliver seated at the counter. He'd given up alcohol for a large cup of tea. I had to admit I was kind of glad he had. We didn't need a bunch of drunk people grieving and agitated and trapped together in a blizzard. That seemed like a recipe for disaster. And honestly, things weren't going that well already.

"Hey there," I said gently. "How are you doing?"

He shrugged, then stared down into his mug. "I'm alright. I just can't really wrap my mind around what's happened. Sienna dead. It just doesn't make sense."

Normally, I would tell Oliver about what I found in the guest-house, but he didn't want to believe that Sienna could be involved in drugs again, and it wasn't like I knew for certain. So, it just seemed cruel to upset him further. I did however feel like I could share what George told me about Rage and Sienna.

"Did you notice anything unusual going on between Sienna and Rage this week?"

Oliver frowned. "Not really. Why?"

"George Sprague, one of our regulars, said that he overheard Rage and Madeline arguing, and it sounded like it was about Sienna. He thought Madeline found them in some sort of compromising position."

Oliver looked unconvinced. "I didn't notice anything going on. But Sienna is—was always a shameless flirt. We all know that."

Yes, we did know that, but I never thought her behavior with men was ever quite as harmless as Oliver made it sound. Yes, she did flirt but I always felt that if the flirting went further, Sienna wouldn't have said no. I hated to think she would do that to a friend, but I knew she would. Truthfully, Oliver did, too, but I could understand him wanting to romanticize her memory. That was natural when someone lost a friend or loved one. And I didn't want to ruin that for him.

Oliver took a sip of his tea and then set it down and I could tell a thought had come to him. "Actually, now that you mention it, Madeline was really ticked off at the slopes one day this week, but I didn't really give it much thought. Mads can be the dingy sweetheart we all know and love. But she can also be quite moody. There were many times on set when we were doing the original Haley and Jake that she could get downright bratty."

I knew that, too. She had that childish quality, so bratty moments did happen. I'd seen them over the years. And Oliver certainly knew her even better than I did since he worked with her for several years.

"That's true. Even if Sienna did flirt with Rage, Madeline could have just been making more of it than it really was." Even as I said that, my thoughts went back to Rage when we'd been in the shed and how he'd cared for Sienna's body. But that could just be Rage being a caring, grief-stricken friend.

"Yeah, I think that was all it was. Mads being Mads," he said, as if that situation were resolved. "Honestly, Rage and Madeline are crazy about each other."

I still wasn't completely convinced that there wasn't more to the story, but I nodded.

There was a rap on the door, and I called for the person to come in. It was Justin.

Oliver perked up a little bit at the sight of our handsome sheriff. "Hey there, Sheriff Pelletier. Long time no see."

Justin nodded to my friend. "It's good to see you again, Oliver. I'm sorry it's under these circumstances."

Oliver sighed. "Yeah, it really is a bit of a drag." He chuckled humorlessly. "Actually, that's a major understatement."

Justin nodded sympathetically, remaining silent for a moment, then he turned to me. "I'm going to have to head out. I just wanted to let you know that you can call me if you need anything. I also told everyone who is still in the pub to just stay put. It's just not safe out there."

"I have plenty of space here for everyone to spend the night, so we should be fine." No sooner did I say that, the lights flickered. Thankfully, just for a moment.

Justin looked up at the overhead light in the kitchen. "You do have a generator for the pub, don't you?"

I groaned, remembering that I still hadn't asked Dave about the generator. "Yes, but I'm not sure it's filled with gas. Actually, I do need to go check on that." I turned to Oliver. "Do you want to come with me down to the pub?"

Oliver gestured to his cup of tea. "I'm going to finish this and then I'll be down."

Once we reached the bottom of the stairs, I said quietly, "Justin, I found some things in the guesthouse amongst Sienna's stuff. I think they might indicate she was using drugs."

I reached into my coat pocket and pulled out the rubber tubing I'd found. I held it up for him to see. Jack, who was still by the coats, blinked lazily at us.

"I'm not really sure what this is, but doesn't it look like something that could be used if you are injecting drugs?" I asked.

Justin inspected the neon tube. "I can't say that I've ever seen anything like this, but yeah, it does look like you could use it to tie off your arm. What else did you find?"

"In her toiletry bag, I saw something that looked like a syringe."

Justin raised an eyebrow to that. "Well, it sounds very possible that this was some sort of accidental overdose. Once they do an autopsy, we will know for sure." Justin looked toward the door. "I really do have to go. One of my officers called, and there is a logging truck off the road on Route 1. No injuries but there are logs across the road. It's definitely safer here than it is outside, that's for sure. But just give me a call if you need anything." He opened the door to my front porch and headed outside.

Jack backed away from the rush of cold. He was no fool. He wanted to stay in here, too.

I locked the door behind Justin, really hoping what he said was true. I definitely hoped we were safe here and that there wasn't an actual murderer on the loose.

FIVE

"DAVE HAS BEEN over there talking to your redheaded friend for like the past twenty minutes," Brandy announced as soon as I walked into the pub. She shot a suspicious look at the table where they sat. "There's just something about her. It rubs me the wrong way."

I watched them for a moment. Madeline was clearly talking a mile a minute, and Dave was hanging on her every word. Madeline reached across the table and rested her hand on Dave's. Even from this distance, I could see his reaction. Dave was half in love already. It did bother me that Madeline seemed oblivious to the effect she was having on him. Either that, or she liked it.

"Where's Rage?"

"Rage," Brandy snorted. All week, she'd been remarking on the ridiculousness of his name. She shrugged. "I haven't seen him for a while."

That seemed weird. Where would he be? Then I noticed Brett was gone, too. "Where's Brett?"

Brandy made another face. "Mr. Obnoxious has found a friend." She jerked her head toward the kitchen.

Brett befriended Jimmy? That seemed like an unlikely friend-ship. I headed to the kitchen, but instead of finding Brett chattering away to the silent cook, I found him hanging out in the dish area with Henry. They leaned on the stainless steel counter, sharing a bottle of whiskey, while chuckling like old friends.

Well, that actually made more sense.

"Have you seen Rage?" I asked Brett.

Brett grimaced at me like I was his mother breaking up his teenage basement party. "He might have gone out to the guesthouse."

Might? I found it hard to believe Henry was so engaging that Brett hadn't noticed his friend going out into the blizzard of the decade. And why would Rage go out there?

Just then, the kitchen door swung open, caught by the wind. I jumped and Brett and his new buddy laughed as if my reaction was the funniest thing in the world. I glared at them. Brett didn't notice, but Henry did. He smiled almost smugly. Thankfully, I had my Indeed Help Wanted ad saved on my phone.

Rage stumbled into the room, blankets and pillows mounted up in his arms so that he could barely see around them. I stepped forward to take some of them.

"I thought I'd get the bedding so people can crash in the main house," Rage explained. "Mads refuses to go back out to the guesthouse."

I hadn't counted on them expecting to stay in my house. It wasn't like Sienna had been found dead *there*. I had four bedrooms in the main house. That wasn't enough space for all the people trapped here. But I didn't want to be insensitive, so I nodded. "We'll find room for everyone."

"Fun," Henry said, eyeing me in a way that made my skin crawl. "A slumber party."

Eww. "Actually, Henry, you can head home if you want. You said you lived nearby, right?"

"Well, that cop said we should stay put." He smiled that unnervingly smug smile again.

I didn't respond, instead turning back to Rage. "Let's put this stuff down in the pub."

I left the kitchen, wanting to get away from both Henry and Brett—the Jerk Twins. I felt bad leaving Jimmy with them.

"I don't like that guy," Rage said as we piled the bedding on one of the pub tables.

"Which one?" I said wryly.

Rage chuckled. "Valid. I think Brett has gotten worse with age. And I thought he was an annoying teenager."

I kind of had to agree.

"But I was actually referring to your employee. Henry?"

I nodded. Although he wasn't going to be my employee after tonight.

"I saw him out near the guesthouse. He acted all shifty when I asked him what he was doing."

"Really?" So he did know where Rage was when I asked. Why had he played dumb? "Do you think he'd gone inside?"

"No, I don't think so. I looked for signs of snow around the door or wet footprints and I didn't see anything. But he's just really weird. He's been lurking around outside all day even with all this snow. It just doesn't make any sense to me."

His behavior didn't make any sense to me either, and he definitely gave me tons of negative vibes. As someone who lived by the motto "good vibes only," I wasn't exactly thrilled that he was snowed in with us.

"Also, earlier today he cornered Madeline. As soon as I walked up to them, he left. I asked her what he was talking to her about and she just laughed it off and said that he was a fan, asking about Hollywood and things like that. I just didn't get a good feeling about it." Rage glanced over to the table where Madeline still sat with Dave. "Unlike your goofy bartender. Now, he seems like a good guy, and he's clearly got a huge crush on Madeline."

I was glad to see that Rage wasn't taking Dave's attention to his girlfriend for anything more than what it was. A harmless crush.

"Dave is a little smitten with Mads. But you're right, he's a great guy and totally harmless."

The lights flickered again, once more reminding me that I still needed to check on the generator situation. "I actually need to talk to Dave about our generator. I've been meaning to do it all day but I keep getting sidetracked."

Rage laughed dryly. "Yes, I can safely say this has been one of the strangest days of my life."

I gave him a sympathetic smile not sure what to say. Mostly, I hoped the night went much better. Which meant keeping lights and heat. As I walked over to Dave, I noticed that Oliver had returned to the bar, and of all things, he was chatting with Brandy. In fact, they seemed to be in a rather deep conversation—and I didn't see a hint of snarkiness flying between the two of them. I blinked. I think they even just smiled at each other. The sight cheered me up a little. I very much wanted them to be friends since I loved them both.

Then I spotted the female half of the odd couple still sat in the corner. She was alone. I glanced around to see where her grouchy counterpart was. Maybe he left his phone long enough to run to the restroom. The woman was talking on her phone, while also working on her laptop. Although I couldn't hear what she was saying, she was definitely more animated than I'd seen her thus far. Work must be going well. I could guarantee if the power went out and we had no generator, there were going to be some complaints from that table.

"Hey, Dave, could I talk to you for a minute?" I could have just asked him about the generator while he sat with Madeline, but there was a protective part of me that didn't want him getting his hopes up by spending too much time with her. I knew Dave was a big boy and he could handle his own feelings, but he really had a sweet, naive quality that made me want to shield him. Dave glanced at me, then back to Madeline, clearly not wanting to leave her, but he nodded and stood up.

"Thank you, Dave, for keeping me company," Madeline said, smiling adorably.

She certainly seemed to be feeling much better, so perhaps the talk with Dave had been a good thing.

"Oh no, please, the pleasure was definitely all mine," Dave said with a slight, gentlemanly bow. Dave really was so cute. He did need a nice—and actually available—girlfriend. I needed to add him to my matchmaking list along with Brandy.

Madeline giggled and ran a hand through her bright auburn hair. The waves fell back into place perfectly. I could practically see cartoon hearts dancing in Dave's eyes as he walked toward me. *Oh Dave.*

"So hey," I said, trying to bring him back to reality. "Dean asked me to ask you about the generator." I left out the part where that was actually hours ago. "He said that you worked on getting it ready for the winter."

Dave's dreamy expression faded completely, replaced by one of awkward consternation. "Oh right, the generator. You know, I did look at it. A few weeks ago. And it was running well."

"Okay, that all sounds great. So, why do I get the feeling there is more to this story?"

"Well, like I said, I did look at it," Clearly, he was repeating that for good measure. "I just might not have remembered to get more propane." He winced with regret.

"Exactly how much propane do you think we have?" Dean said, appearing beside me, catching the last bit of our conversation. He didn't look pleased.

Dave's eyes looked off to the side as he considered Dean's question. "I'd say a solid—half a tank."

Dean looked even less pleased.

"Sorry," Dave said immediately. "I totally forgot. Plus, that was during the time I was dating Melanie and she was really demanding. And so bossy. So, I just don't feel like I was really on my game. I know it's not a good reason, but—"

Dean raised a hand to stop him. "It's okay."

Dave shoved his hands in his jeans pockets, looking like an ashamed little boy. Well, a little boy in a Grateful Dead tie-dye t-shirt and with a man bun. I personally believed his reason for forgetting about the generator. Dating Melanie had been a confusing time in his life. I thought he dodged a bullet with that one.

"I'm going to go take a look at it and see what kind of shape we're in," Dean said.

"I'll go with you," Dave offered.

I could tell Dean would actually prefer to handle it alone, but he nodded. "Sure."

Dean probably wanted to add something about it being more help if Dave had just finished the job to begin with. But Dean was a great manager, and he knew Dave, in general, was a reliable and conscientious employee, so he wasn't going to berate him for one mistake. Although it might turn out to be a big one if we lost power. I had no clue how long a half a tank of propane would last, but given Dean's expression, not long. But I couldn't say anything. I'd been distracted and forgetting things all day. And I didn't even have pushy Melanie to blame. But I suppose a friend dying was a valid excuse, too.

Speaking of forgetfulness, I still needed to go out to the barn and get some food for Jack. I was afraid to even go check on him. I had images of chewed-up coats strewn everywhere. Jack could get hangry.

I dreaded going out there, but I couldn't very well ask anyone else to do it. I knew Dean would, but he had been handling so much around here that I didn't want to add to his stress. If I just bundled up and put my head down, literally, it wouldn't take that long. What's a little frostbite for your beloved pet?

"Brandy," I said, approaching the bar. "I have to go out to Jack's shed. I forgot to bring in his food."

Both Brandy and Oliver looked highly opposed to the idea.

"Can't you just feed Jack a couple of salads out of the kitchen?" Oliver said.

It wasn't a bad idea. Although I'd probably have to feed him all of our stock to fill him up for the night. Plus, Jack could have a sensitive stomach and lettuce didn't always sit well. Visions of something other than shredded outerwear all over the hallway floor came to mind. I shuddered. I loved having a pet—I was not a fan of cleaning up after one.

"He would love that, but it's no big deal to run out to the barn. It'll be quick."

Oliver stood up. "Okay, it's time for me to get manly here. I'm going with you. Just wait for me to grab my coat and gloves."

"I appreciate the offer, but it's honestly not necessary." I wasn't sure if he knew that we'd placed Sienna in the barn. But I knew that he couldn't handle seeing her like that. He was calmer now, I didn't want to harsh his mellow. Plus, I thought manly might be overreaching to describe Oliver. "Just stay here and have a hot cocoa waiting for me." I pulled up my hood. "I'm already in my coat, and it really will only take me a couple seconds."

Seconds was an exaggeration, of course. Wading through snow wasn't a speed sport. But I certainly planned to make it as quick as possible. This was not a night fit for man nor beast. Now I finally understood the expression. It suited a Maine nor'easter perfectly. "Actually, make it a hot cocoa with a shot of Cointreau."

I still stood by my theory that drinking too much in this situation could go horribly wrong, but one shot to warm up seemed reasonable.

"Mmm, chocolate and orange." Oliver's eyes lit up. "That does sound yummy. Count me in."

I chuckled as I tugged on my gloves and headed out to the kitchen. It wasn't lost on me that I hadn't exactly had to twist Oliver's arm to convince him to stay behind. But he was even more of a California-dreaming sort than I was.

As soon as I pushed through the kitchen door, I was hit by two things at once—the kitchen smelled delicious, but unfortunately, chummy Brett and Henry were still working on their bromance and sharing a bottle of whiskey. Now, they sat on one of the metal prep counters. Which would have to be properly disinfected thanks to their butts.

I ignored them and turned to my cook. "Jimmy, what are you making? It smells delicious."

I started to head over to take a peek into the large stewpot he had simmering, fully not expecting an answer. But to my surprise, my grumpy cook said in a gravelly voice that I'm sure was rusty from lack of use, "Chili. I got potatoes and cornbread baking. I reckon we got to feed all these folks."

That was true. We were all here for the night, and actually, the idea of having everyone together to share a meal seemed like a good plan. We needed to do something to make this strange situation less dreary.

I glanced at Brett and Henry. Maybe, if we were lucky, those two would pass out before we sat down to eat. I knew that wasn't very generous of me. I liked to consider myself a tolerant person, but today has been stressful. And frankly, they were getting on my nerves.

Brett laughed loudly, just to validate my point. Aside from a brief clench of my teeth, I ignored him.

"Thank you, Jimmy. That sounds perfect, and it's a huge help."

I shot a pointed look at Henry, hoping he might get the hint. A pile of dishes still waited to be run through the dishwasher. If he was going to stay, he could at least do his job. Especially since he was drinking on the job. Was it too much to ask for him to drink and wash?

He didn't pick up on my signal, whatsoever, too busy telling Brett a dirty joke.

I sighed. "Alright, I'm heading out to get some food for my llama." I crossed to the backdoor, then stopped to add, "Brandy and Oliver know where I am, so they'll send out the troops if I'm missing for too long."

I glanced at Henry. I wasn't totally sure why, but I felt like he, specifically, needed to know that. He smiled, then took a swig of his whiskey.

"I don't get you and that llama," Brett said, his words already slurring.

"She's a llama mama, dude," Henry said, his words also a little sloppy. They both guffawed as if that was the most hilarious thing that had ever been said. But on an up note, if their speech was any indication, I might get my wish and they'd be unconscious under a table somewhere by the time the cornbread was out of the oven.

I pulled my hood tighter around my face and stepped out into the storm. I think I might actually prefer driving wind and snow over those two. I was also pleased that I was actually getting better at navigating the deep snow. I only got stuck once, nearly losing my boot as I yanked my foot out of a thigh-high drift. But I forged on. Creepy Henry was actually right. I was a llama mama. A proud one, darn it.

Fortunately, the fence gate and the barn door were still movable, at least enough to squeeze through, and I was soon in the shed. I leaned against the door, catching my breath. I was doing better with the balance and speed, but I was still struggling with the endurance part of deep-snow walking.

Keeping my eyes averted from the place where Sienna was lying, I headed straight to the feed barrel. Crud, I should have brought some sort of bag for the pellets, and something for the hay, too. I scanned the barn, trying to find something I could use, still avoiding looking at Sienna's shrouded body. I spotted another wool blanket. I could wrap up some of the hay in that, and on the other side of the shed, there was a metal pail. Unfortunately, it was also on the other side of Sienna.

Okay, let's just do this. The sooner I got the food, the sooner I could leave.

"Not that I'm not enjoying your company," I said to Sienna. I figured it couldn't hurt to cover my bases. You know, in case she was lurking around in spirit form. If she was earthbound, I didn't think she'd be Sienna the Friendly Ghost. I wasn't taking any chances.

I risked a glance at her, just to be sure there was no ectoplasm or mist swirling around her body. Immediately, I could feel the blood drain from my frigid cheeks and my limbs grew even colder, if that was possible.

There was no ghost, but I could see her whole body, still positioned on top of the blanket. Which was definitely better than a ghost, except I knew I shouldn't be able to see her at all. Rage had covered her up before we left. But now she was totally unwrapped, her hands crossed on her stomach just as Rage had positioned her. At least she hadn't moved. Just the blanket. That was something, right?

I glanced at the door nervously. Maybe the wind had blown the blanket open, but I knew that wasn't possible. Yes, it was windy, and there was a draft in the shed but certainly not enough breeze to move a heavy, wool, horse blanket.

I looked at the door again, chills making me shiver and not just because of the subzero temperatures. Tentatively, I took a step toward the body, forcing myself to take a closer look at her, but I stopped, unable to make myself get too close. Images of her pulling a Carrie and grabbing my legs flashed in my head. Oliver would tell me this was why a person should never, ever watch a horror movie.

She didn't appear to have been disturbed in any way. Her skin looked paler and more waxy, and her dark hair was white with ice, but other than the blanket being pulled away from her, she looked the same.

So, who would come in here and unwrap her like that? Maybe Justin had come out before he left. I did tell him about the drug theory, so he could have decided to check her for needle marks or something. But would he have bothered to pose her in the same position Rage had, yet not cover her again? Also, he'd been in a rush to get back to his officers. I got the feeling that he just planned to get her body transferred to the coroner's and let them handle determining the cause of death. So, Justin didn't make any sense.

One thing was for sure, I wasn't going to stand out here analyzing all the possibilities of what might have happened. The lights flickered as if to tell me to hurry up. That was all the warning I needed.

I scurried past Sienna, giving both her and the blanket a wide berth, and snatched up the pail. I skirted the body again and grabbed a blanket that was hanging on the wall. With both hands up, I shoveled several mounds of hay onto the center of the mostly spread-out blanket. Then I folded in the four corners to make a makeshift bundle. Outside the wind gusted, and the shed creaked. I spared a quick glance at Sienna. She was still lying there.

Okay, Oliver, you win. No horror movies ever again.

I had to get a grip. This was Sienna, after all. Even if she did somehow rise from the dead, it wasn't like she was going to attack me and eat my brains. I looked at her again. Actually, I wasn't totally sure about that.

I grabbed the pail and ladled several scoopfuls of food pellets into it. Then with the pail in one hand and the bundle in the other, swung over my shoulder like Santa Claus, I headed to the door.

Jack had better appreciate this. This definitely went above and beyond, even for the best llama mama. For a second, I paused, debating if I should wrap Sienna up again.

I decided not to bother. It wasn't as if the blanket was needed to keep her warm. Plus, I had a feeling that if the tables were turned, she wouldn't have gone back to wrap me up. Truth be told, she probably would have left me in the snowbank. So I think we were good here.

Walking was much harder with my hands full, and I struggled to keep my balance. It seemed like it took forever to make it to the fence, and as I shoved my way through the gate, I lost my footing and fell forward. The blanket bundle wedged between the fence and the gate, catching on the latch and stopping me from landing on my face. Some of the food pellets spilled over the top of the pail onto the snow.

I cursed, which I had to say, I had done more that day than I'd done in the last year. Usually, my rare curse words were reserved for stubbing my toe or bumping my elbow. This evening was beating the pants off of both of those things for being highly unpleasant.

Reining in my irritation and gathering my strength, I used the fence to get myself back on my feet. Thankfully, the blanket tugged off the latch easily and I started moving again, only to stop once more. For the first time, I realized there were a set of tracks in the snow that split off from mine. My tracks headed toward the back of the pub, while the other set went toward the other side of my house, and I assumed, around the front. It was too dark and there was too much snow blowing around me to see where they led for certain.

Snow had also started filling in the prints nearest to me, but they were still clear. As if whoever made them had been out here not too long before me.

I hiked the bundle up on my shoulder and awkwardly retraced my own footprints, hoping that would allow me to go quicker. I did not want to be out here any longer than I had to be.

And not just because I was freezing.

SIX

"YOU MADE IT BACK," Oliver said, raising a mug in my direction. "Your hot chocolate awaits."

I held up the bucket and blanket. "Let me finish getting Jack situated, and I'll be back."

Oliver raised the mug again in toast. "We'll be waiting."

He turned back to chatting with Brandy. They laughed about something, and I felt oddly left out. He'd probably spent more time chatting with her than he had with me since he arrived.

But I was definitely glad Oliver felt better.

When I walked into the hallway, Jack was still standing near the hooks draped with outerwear. "Hey there, buddy, Still hanging with the coats. I didn't realize you had a jacket obsession."

I set down the pail and blanket and then went to see what had him so fascinated. Maybe I'd hung up a coat that still had a peppermint in the pocket. He rivaled a black Friday shopper waiting in line to score a cheap TV when it came to holding out for his favorite treat.

As I stopped beside him, he poked his nose against one coat in particular. It wasn't one of mine. Some of my grandmother's sweaters and coats still hung on the hooks. When I'd inherited her house, it came with all her stuff, too. I hadn't had the heart to even move any of it. Seeing all her stuff right where she'd hung it, somehow made me feel closer to her.

Jack nuzzled the jacket again. It was one that looked like she'd worn it when she was out working in her garden. There was a smudge of dirt on the sleeve and I could picture her kneeling in the rich, spring soil planting all her amazing flowers.

My llama snuffled the garment again, making a loud snort. Then he rumbled. His happy rumble.

He could smell my grandmother, I suddenly realized.

"Do you miss Grammy?"

As if to answer me, he nudged the garment again. The sight of him smelling the coat of his previous owner hit me like a sucker punch. It never dawned on me that maybe Jack missed my grandmother. But why wouldn't he? Animals had feelings too. Then I marveled how strange it was that a llama had known my own grandmother better than I did.

I hugged Jack around the neck, a wave of melancholy washing over me. I missed my hippie grandmother too, even though I barely knew her. But from what I did know of Sunny, I loved her. Her sense of style, her wild flower garden, her gorgeous, eclectic home.

I also felt heartsick about Sienna. Sure, she'd had more than her fair share of unlikable traits, but she had been my friend for years. It was hard to believe she was really gone. And it was even harder to understand *why* she was gone. This didn't feel like a simple drug overdose.

After seeing her body uncovered, I had an even stronger feeling that her death was more suspicious than I had even originally thought.

I hugged Jack tighter and he rumbled. Then he turned his long neck and nibbled at my hair. I smiled.

"Okay, buddy. I'm going to make you up a bed and get you some food and water." I told him as I headed up my stairs. "And maybe even a peppermint."

Jack made a deep purring noise.

"Sweet talker," I called back to him.

. . .

"WHAT THE HAY took you so long?" Oliver said as soon as I returned into the pub. "Get it, hay? I amuse myself so much."

"Had to get Jack settled and then I needed to change. My pants were soaked through from the snow."

I collapsed onto the barstool next to him and he slid a mug of hot cocoa toward me. I took a long sip, groaning with satisfaction. "Oh, that is good."

My muscles already ached from my many adventures outside today. I could only imagine how sore I was going to be tomorrow. "I think I could start a lucrative side gig doing blizzard workouts. I've done everything from hot yoga to extreme cycling class and, frankly, I've never felt the burn like trudging through thigh-high snow."

"Time to relax, then," Oliver said, clinking his mug against mine and then Brandy's. "But you're right. Make fake snow in L.A. and bill it as a workout and you'd make millions."

Oliver leaned back on his stool to admire my sweatpants and slouchy bright blue sweatshirt. "You do look comfy. Or like you might start breakdancing. What a feeling. Keep believing." He grinned.

I stuck my tongue out at him, but did tug up my neckline, which very Flashdance-esque had slipped down on my shoulder.

"I'm personally jealous. You look ridiculously comfy."

"I am. Thank you," I said, primly. "If you want to borrow something, just let me know."

Brandy glanced down at her own tight, skinny jeans. "I just might."

"So what's been going on here?" I asked.

"Everyone is pretty much settling in to ride out the storm," Brandy said, taking a sip of her wine. Brandy never drank on the job, but tonight didn't count. Other than the aloof couple in the corner, everyone trapped here was friends. Actually, I might add Brett and Henry to the not-quite-friend list, too.

"Riders on the storm," Oliver sang in his best Jim Morrison voice. He looked around. "Man, you need a jukebox in here."

"That would be nice," I agreed. Maybe, I should have sprung for that rather than a big-screen TV. Although the television was paying off. We were getting decent crowds in here to watch sporting events. The locals loved their Pats and Celtics. Dean assured me the Red Soxs would be a huge draw too. I glanced up at the screen. Joe Stalling was still on, predicting the end times. At least he was now muted.

"Can we get a music channel on the TV?" I asked, which goes to show how much I'd even fiddled with the new flat screen.

"Good thought," Brandy said, pulling out the remote from under the bar. She turned and started flipping through the channels.

"Doesn't the remote have a guide or something?" Oliver said, watching stations flip by.

Brandy studied the remote. "I don't know."

On the screen, was an image of a deserted town street engulfed by swirling snow and two-foot drifts. A headline on the scene read, *The Ski Trip From Hell.*

Well, that certainly was apropos to the situation we were in. If my friends had thought their trip was bad before, Sienna's sudden demise and the blizzard would put this trip at the top of all their worst vacation lists. Before I could see anything more about the new story, or whatever it was, Brandy found the button to pull up the guide.

"Here we go," she said, scrolling through the grid of channels. "What do you think? Should we go with the nineties station? You know, in honor of the last time this pub was remodeled."

"Hey!" I protested. "We have a flat screen. Nothing nineties about that."

"You can never go wrong with nineties music," Oliver said.

That seemed like a sweeping statement to me, but I wasn't going to protest.

Brandy clicked on the appropriate station and turned up the

volume. The familiar voices of Destiny's Child filled the pub. The song was just ending and it immediately went straight into the Backstreet Boys. We all started to imitate standard boy band dance movements along with the beat of the song. It was impossible not to do so. Even Dave sitting on the bar talking to George, joined in.

I had to admit that the music was exactly what we needed.

"I love this song." Madeline appeared beside us. She slid on a barstool next to me and Rage also joined us. "I had such a crush on Nick in grade school."

"Everyone did," Brandy assured her.

The music made the whipping winds outside seem a little less daunting and the pub seemed a little more cozy. I think we all need the distraction from that and even more so the heaviness of Sienna's death.

George Sprague suddenly yelled out, "Turn this crap off! My ears are bleeding."

Okay, so maybe not everyone was into boy bands or reassured by a pounding bass beat.

"Chill, dude," Dave told him. "Majority rules, man."

Everyone else ignored George.

Celine Dion started crooning that she was his lady and he was her man, which prompted Brandy to pull out her cell phone.

"Hey," she said to Oliver, "remember that guy I told you about. The FBI agent I've been texting with?"

Oliver quickly swallowed his sip of cocoa, nodding.

"Maybe I could get your take on his texts. I mean, I know he's interested, but I'd love to hear what you think." Brandy opened her phone, getting ready to take Oliver down her silver fox rabbit-hole.

Somehow, I didn't think she was really going to like hearing Oliver's opinion on them. Oliver wasn't quite as gentle with his feedback as I was. He was actually brutally honest.

I turned on my barstool, deciding this would be a good time to see how the odd couple in the corner were doing. "I'll be right back." Yes, I was fleeing. I was a little worried that Brandy and

Oliver's newly developed friendship was about to hit its first rocky patch.

"Hey there," I said, attempting to be overly friendly again with the couple. And yet again, I was greeted by a less than warm reception. Although the man didn't actually scowl at me this time. Maybe I was making headway. He shifted in his seat.

"Can I get you anything to drink?" Then I noticed the bottle of champagne on their table. "Oh, it looks like you are all set."

The woman nodded. I actually saw a glimmer of something that might be excitement in her dark eyes. Or maybe she was nervous. I couldn't really tell.

"Yes," the man—Bryce—said. "The server now seated on the bar over there, having a drink, has been checking on us." I didn't miss his disdain for my relaxing staff, which rubbed me the wrong way.

"You will have to excuse my staff's casualness tonight. Since we are all stuck here, I'm loosening the rules a bit. Snow days are the time to break the rules, right?" I quoted Janelle.

Uptight Bryce didn't look convinced, but the woman smiled. Another of those forced numbers that looked more like a grimace than an actual friendly gesture. Her cell phone rang and she actually jumped. The man eyed it, too. The woman tapped the screen, sending the caller to voicemail.

They both looked uncomfortable. Something was so up with these two.

"So, what are you celebrating?" I asked. That's right. I wasn't going anywhere until I got at least a little information out of these two.

"We had a huge break at work," the woman answered readily. "Like huge."

Bryce shot her a warning look, and the woman snapped her mouth shut. She took a sip of her champagne.

"Well, that's great. You never did say what you do for work."

"No, we didn't." Jerky Bryce scowled.

The woman polished off her champagne and reached for the bottle. Clearly, neither of them was going to volunteer anything.

"Okay, well, you two are actually our only patrons tonight, so feel free to ask any of us if you need something."

"We will," scowling Bryce said, and I could tell I was being dismissed.

I started to turn away from them, when I noticed that the legs of his pants were damp, the gray wool now black up to his knees. And his expensive Oxfords were soaked. That Italian leather wasn't going to make a recovery anytime soon.

"Did you venture out into the storm?"

He glanced down to where I was looking. "Oh—yeah," His hesitant response was the first time I'd seen any signs of any reaction other than rudeness. "I went out to try to get our car out of the snow, but it's definitely stuck."

The woman nodded. She took another drink, hiding her expression behind the champagne flute.

There was no doubt in my mind these two were shifty and hiding something. I considered offering to find him some dry socks or something, but he scowled at me--again--and I rejected the idea. My kindness had its limits.

"We will be serving dinner soon. So just let me know if you need anything before then." This time, I didn't wait for a reply. I knew it would be just another arrogant grimace from Seriously Rude Bryce.

"Brandy, you always text him first," Oliver said, still looking at her phone. "He's just answering you back."

Uh-oh. Oliver was giving it to her straight, and I could tell by the narrowing of Brandy's eyes, she was not going to go for that. This was definitely a good time to interrupt.

"Hey," I said, placing both hands on the bar to lean over it and draw their attention to me. I kept my voice low, although I didn't think the corner-couple could hear me over Madonna, urging us to express ourselves. I didn't want Brandy to do that right now. Not when she was clearly getting hot. "Did any of you see that guy in the corner go outside earlier?"

Brandy glanced down at her phone, but then shoved it into her back pocket and nodded.

"Yeah, I did. He went out before you went to get Jack's food."

"How long before?"

She shrugged. "I'm not totally sure. Why?"

I hesitated for a moment. All the Cali friends were feeling a bit better, and I wasn't sure if I should bring up anything about Sienna.

"I was just curious. Actually, Brandy, would you mind helping me move some of the tables together to make one big table? Jimmy made chili and some other sides, so I was thinking it would be nice if we all had a family-style meal together. It will be a good distraction from everything going on tonight."

"I can help," Oliver said, but I immediately shook my head, giving him a warning look.

He frowned, and I don't think he understood what I was warning him against. But he shrugged. Fortunately, Rage was on his phone and didn't hear me. And Madeline was gone. Probably in the bathroom or something.

"Yeah, I can help." Brandy came around the bar, but not before she shot Oliver an irritated glance. Oliver had moved on to checking his own phone. He had no idea that I'd just saved him from Brandy's wrath. She'd worked very hard on creating her epic romance between herself and FBI Agent Mark Winters, and even a newly blossoming friendship was not going to temper her elaborate fantasy.

Dave jumped down the bar. "Hey, I can help you guys."

Brandy started to accept his offer, when I cut her off, "That's okay, Dave. Stay where you are. Keep George company. Brandy and I have got this."

Brandy gave me a confused look. It did seem counterproductive to turn down help, but I wanted to talk to Brandy alone. I had to bounce ideas off of someone, and Brandy was a win-win. I'd distract her from her annoyance at Oliver giving her too much hard truth, and I wouldn't have to pull Sienna's other friends into my suspicions.

"Oh man, these tables are heavy," I groaned, trying to wiggle it side to side toward another one.

"Da—" Brandy started to call to her coworker.

I raised a hand to stop her. "I need to talk to you alone."

"Never mind, Dave."

Dave shook his head, clearly having no idea what was going on. Not an unusual state for him.

Brandy took the other side of the table that I was struggling to move. "Did you want to talk to me about the fact that Oliver has no idea what is romantic? You know, I remember you saying that he has trouble keeping his relationships going, and now, I totally understand why. He's absolutely oblivious to any sort of romantic undertone between two people. I bet his boyfriends just give up because he is so obtuse."

"No, not about that," I said, still managing to be noncommittal about FBI Agent Silver Fox—and now her theory on why Oliver's relationships never lasted long. "Actually, I wanted to talk to you about something that I saw in the shed."

Her disgruntled expression immediately changed to one of curiosity. I hadn't actually thought she'd drop her analysis of Oliver's inability to gauge true romance quite so quickly. Her love of a good mystery seemed to usurp her obsession with her FBI agent. Or annoyance with Oliver. She moved closer to me.

"What was it?" she whispered, her eyes alight with the thrill of potential clues.

"When we put Sienna in Jack's barn, Rage actually positioned the body like it would be in a casket, and then he carefully wrapped her up in a wool blanket."

Brandy pulled back from me, making a mildly disgusted face. "Okay, I mean, I guess I might do the same thing."

She didn't sound or look convincing.

"I have to admit I found his behavior a little strange. It's not like he and Sienna were super tight. In fact, he's the one person who has known her the shortest amount of time. But Rage has always been a super kind-hearted guy, so it's possible he would have done that for anyone."

"His name definitely doesn't suit him," Brandy agreed. "Although I'm not sure the name Rage would really suit anybody." She thought for a brief second. "I don't know, maybe a superhero or super villain, I guess. Possibly a deejay."

"The thing is," I said, cutting off her name analysis, "it's not really Rage's behavior that has me curious—well, it kind of does. But what is really weird is the fact that when I went out there to get Jack's food, Sienna's body was totally unwrapped from the blanket. It didn't look as if her body was moved in any way, but she was uncovered. There was no way wind could have done that."

Brandy gave me a curious look. "So other than you, who was outside?"

"Rage did go to the guesthouse to get extra bedding for tonight. I have no idea how long he was out there. So, it's possible he could have done it."

Brandy nodded, then frowned. "But why? It doesn't make any sense that he would go to the trouble of arranging and covering her body just to sneak in and uncover it."

"That's true. Unless he went back to the body to look for something and got disturbed. He did also tell me that he saw Henry outside. But he said Henry was near the guesthouse."

"And he could just as easily have told you he saw Henry at the barn. That would have been the perfect cover for Rage, if he had been out there looking for something. We all think Henry is a creep."

That was true.

"Where is Janelle?" I said, suddenly realizing she wasn't hanging out at the bar. I didn't think she had been outside. I was more worried she was being harassed by the drunken Jerk Twins in the kitchen.

"She's probably chatting with her grandfather."

"Grandfather?" What the heck was Brandy talking about?

"Jimmy is Janelle's granddad." Brandy gave me a duh look.

I gaped at her. I'd known both Jimmy and Janelle almost since the moment I arrived in Friendship Harbor months ago and I had no idea they were related. "How did I not know this?"

Brandy shrugged. "I have no idea."

Wow, that really made me question my sleuthing abilities and power of observation. I blinked, then tried to return to our original topic. "Dean and Dave were outside around the same time, checking the generator but neither of them would have any reason to disturb Sienna's body." I paused. "Really, Jimmy is Janelle's grandfather?"

Brandy laughed. "Yes."

Okay, that was nuts. I'd never even imagined Jimmy having a life outside of the pub, let alone kids and grandkids.

"Maybe Dave or Dean did go out there. Maybe they were looking for something." Brandy didn't sound any more convinced by the idea than I was.

"Like what? You know Dean, he's not into all my mystery-solving. He thinks I make more out of everything than there really is." Which thus far hadn't been the case. But apparently, I did miss things that were right in front of me. Jimmy and Janelle. Related. I think my mind was officially blown.

"Dave definitely wouldn't go out there," Brandy said decisively, and I agreed. The Grateful Dead was definitely as close to dead as our hippie millennial wanted to get.

"But maybe they did see something or someone while they were out there." I glanced at Dave. He was still talking to George, motioning with his hands as if he was casting out a fishing line and reeling it back in. Who knew what was going on there.

"Have you seen Dean?" I asked suddenly. Wow, I was off my game tonight. I didn't even notice that he was missing. Maybe I'd gotten frostbite to the brain.

Brandy shook her head. "Not for awhile."

Okay, that was strange.

"I don't think Brett has been outside since he came over with his luggage," Brandy added.

We managed to line up another of the heavy tables against the ones we had already arranged. "And we know that rude guy in the corner was outside. And not too long before I was. Also, I did see tracks out there that looked relatively fresh to me."

We both cast furtive glances to the couple, then we looked back at each other.

"I think we need to find out more about them," I said. "But first, I need to see where Dean is. It seems weird he isn't here."

Brandy nodded, looking a little worried herself, which only ramped up my concern.

Just then, Rage joined us. "Let me help you. These tables look nearly impossible to move."

"That would be great," Brandy agreed quickly, before I could decline another offer to help. "Go find Dean. We've got this."

I had to admit, I was having an uncomfortable feeling. Dean should have made an appearance by now. Dave had been back since I came down from my place. So, where was Dean?

SEVEN

"DAVE, do you know where Dean is?"

Dave, who was still talking with George Sprague, now stood behind the bar doing moves like a hula dancer. He was telling some story, which from George's wide grin was amusing. I would probably find it amusing too, if I wasn't worried about Dean.

Dave lowered his rhythmically swaying arms. He looked around, clearly noticing for the first time Dean was nowhere to be found. "He was still outside when I came back in. He said he wanted to check the generator for the main house to see if there was more propane in that tank. I told him that I'd help him, but I think I was bugging him, so he sent me back inside."

My part of the house had a generator, too? My interest over that revelation was quickly dismissed as my concern ratcheted up a notch. No one had seen him for easily an hour. Where was he?

Without saying anything else to Dave, I started for the kitchen.

"Soph, is everything okay?" Oliver asked.

"I think Dean is missing." I knew I sounded dramatic, but I felt certain something was wrong.

"Have you checked your phone to see if he texted you?"

I retrieved my phone from my pocket, feeling a little dumb for not thinking of that first. I tapped the screen. Nothing but a severe weather alert. *Great. Thanks for that.* My panic went into overdrive.

"Let me check the kitchen, then Rage and I will check outside." Oliver went to grab his ski parka. I appreciated his offer to go outside. And offering for Rage to go outside too. But Rage didn't seem to mind. He shifted the last table into place for the group dinner with ease. That would have taken Brandy and me twice as long. He jogged over to get his own coat.

"Yeah, we'll go walk around and see if he's still outside." He caught my stricken expression and smiled reassuringly. "I'm sure he's fine. He's got the rugged Maine-guy thing going for him."

I nodded, hoping that was true.

"Yeah," Madeline piped in. "He grew up with all this snow, right? So, I'm sure he's fine."

I regarded her for a moment, trying to decide if she was saying that just to be reassuring or if she somehow knew he was still outside. I was being ridiculous and paranoid. She was just trying to be helpful. She hadn't even been out of the pub since they went to get their luggage hours ago.

"I'm going to go up to my place and see if maybe he's there." He hadn't come into my house when I was changing my clothes, but maybe we just missed each other.

I headed through the stockroom and office to the hallway. When I opened the door, I expected to find Jack settled on his blanket or eating his food, but instead, he stood at the bottom of the stairs. I could tell by the way his ears twitched that he was focused on something.

"Hey, fuzzy guy, what's going on? Is everything okay?"

"I'm pretty sure he thinks I'm dying. He's been hanging over me like a vulture. Llamas are vegetarians, right?"

I raced to the staircase to find Dean half sitting/half sprawled on the steps. His hand was pressed to the back of his head. There was still snow and ice clinging to his wavy, dark hair and even crusted in his eyebrows. He must have just gotten inside.

"Dean!" I stumbled on the stairs in my attempt to get closer to him. His hands shot out to steady me. And protect himself. "Are you okay? What happened? You are half-frozen."

I immediately began poking at his head where his hand had been.

"Hey," he said, wincing and laughing at the same time. "I don't think you're going to win any awards for your nursing skills."

I gentled my touch, but still parted his hair to inspect his head. "Sorry. Oh no, you have a huge lump. What the heck happened?"

"I have no idea." He grimaced as I checked the rest of his scalp.

"Well, clearly something hit you in the head and pretty hard from the looks of it."

"Yeah, that was my deduction too," he said wryly. I made a face at him, but I was glad he felt well enough to be flippant. "The last thing I remember was checking out the generator on the side of your house. And then I woke up in a snowbank."

I gasped. "You passed out? Do you think someone assaulted you?"

He narrowed his eyes, but I wasn't sure if he was trying to recall or his head just hurt. Finally, he said, "I honestly don't know. I don't even know how long I was out. But something had to have really walloped me to actually knock me unconscious."

I shuddered. He could have died out there from hypothermia. "Maybe something was thrown by the wind? Or an icicle maybe. Icicles have killed people, you know."

"Thanks, Mom from A Christmas Story."

It took me a second to get his reference. He'd actually made me watch that movie at Christmastime.

He narrowed his eyes again. He was definitely having trouble focusing.

"You need to see a doctor." I reached into my pocket to get my phone, but he put a hand on my wrist.

"Soph, I'm going to be fine. Nothing a couple of ibuprofen and a hot shower can't fix."

I hesitated, still debating dialing 911. He gently squeezed the wrist he still held. His hand was frozen. He could have literally frozen to death. I suddenly felt sick. Images of tripping over his dead body like I had Sienna's flashed through my mind.

I dropped onto the step beside him. "What if you have a concussion?"

He gave me a crooked grin. "I give you permission to keep me up all night. You know, just to play it safe."

The naughty twinkle in his green-gold eyes made me feel slightly better. And warm all over. Although I did find myself leaning closer to him, trying to see if his pupils were dilated.

"I'm fine," he repeated, realizing what I was doing. He gave me a quick kiss, then he braced a hand on the banister, trying to lever himself onto his feet, only to drop down on his butt again.

Jack, who still stood sentry at the bottom of the stairs, made a noise deep in his chest.

"See, even Jack knows that doesn't look fine." I swiped my phone screen.

"Soph, all emergency services are right out straight tonight."

Right out straight. That meant busy. And I knew he was right. But was it wrong that I was feeling a little swoony at my injured boyfriend's Maine-isms? What can I say? I had a thing for Maine-speak and his accent. I wasn't sure I was supposed to say he was my boyfriend since we'd never had any sort of talk about what we were doing, and we'd just started dating, but in my own head, I was sticking with boyfriend.

But once my little tingly feeling faded, I sighed and nodded. "You're probably right. But I'm going to be watching you, and if you feel worse, I'm calling nine-one-one."

"Sounds reasonable." He gripped the banister again, this time standing up and staying up. "I'm going to take a shower and get into dry clothes."

I rose, too, and looped an arm around his back to steady him. "Let me help you."

He shook his head. "I'm fine. Honestly."

Frustrated, I took a step back. "I don't know who you dated in the past, but it's totally normal to accept help from someone you're seeing. That's kind of part of the deal in relationships."

He paused. "You're right. What can I say? I'm used to being a loner." He gave me a grin, though it looked a little forced. I wasn't sure if that was from the head injury or his fear of letting me breach the walls he had around his heart. "You can tuck me into bed later, how does that sound?"

"Fine. But you will not put up a fight when I give you tea and an ibuprofen and wake you up every two hours to check for a concussion." That was non-negotiable in my book.

He reached the landing. "That's actually very sweet." This time his smile looked more genuine and he reached out and cupped my cheek. "I'm glad you're in my life, Soph."

My heart squeezed. "I'm glad, too. Now, I'll be up to check on you as soon as possible, but first, I've got to let Oliver and Rage know I found you. They are wandering out in the snow as we speak."

His hand drifted down to his side. "Oh, that is not good. Your California pals are definitely in more danger than I am. You definitely better go rescue them."

Dean disappeared up the stairs, and I heard my kitchen door open and close. I turned to Jack, who was also watching Dean from beneath his long lashes. He looked more jealous than concerned, though.

I scruffed his neck, and whispered softly near his ear, "Don't worry, you are always my best boy." I kissed his snout. "But did you hear him? He's glad I'm in his life." I grinned, knowing I looked utterly foolish. I kissed Jack again. "But right now, I have to rescue my friends."

DEAN WAS RIGHT, it was a good thing I went to find Oliver and Rage. Unfortunately, yelling out the kitchen door for them had done no good. The wind raged too loudly, so to my dismay, I had to yet again don my winter clothes and head back outside. They were all the way around the side of my house when I found them. Oliver was swearing up a storm because he had lost his boot and Rage was laughing so hard at his hissy fit that tears were frozen to his cheeks.

"Laugh it up," Oliver grumbled, trying to balance on one foot and lean forward to dig out his boot. Eventually, he got it free and dropped on his butt, sinking into the snow like it was a recliner. He tugged the boot on, still complaining the whole time.

Fortunately, most of Rage's laughter was carried away on the wind.

"Dean is in the house, let's go back inside," I yelled, over the howling of the storm.

It was too frigid to stand around any longer than necessary, so as soon as Oliver was back on his feet, we all stumbled and waded back to the pub.

"Dean better have been in some real distress after all this," Oliver growled once we were in the kitchen.

"He got knocked unconscious, if that makes you feel any better," I informed him.

"Oh crap." Oliver looked up from unzipping his jacket, appropriately shocked. "Okay, I didn't actually want that. Is he alright?"

"Yeah, he's got quite a bump on his head, but I think he'll be fine."

Rage frowned. "Did someone attack him?"

"He has no idea what happened. He might have just fallen and hit his head." I personally found it hard to believe that something just randomly hit him, but I didn't want to get my friends anymore worried or stressed than they already were.

"Somebody attacked your mountain man boyfriend?" Brett slurred, weaving over to us. He pointed the almost empty bottle of whiskey at me. "Now that's some crazy crap right there."

I started to correct him that we actually didn't know what happened, but then realized it was probably pointless. With the amount of alcohol he'd drunk that night, he probably wouldn't remember any of this anyway.

I glanced over to Henry, who still sat on the prep counter. He didn't look nearly as lit as Brett or maybe he was just better at holding his liquor.

"I'm getting hungry," Brett announced suddenly, further proving my point that he probably wouldn't remember anything we'd talked about just now.

"Food is ready," Janelle said from where she worked beside Jimmy, using tongs to put foil-wrapped baked potatoes in a large serving dish. Now that I looked at her and Jimmy together, I could actually see a family resemblance. It was the nose. Although Jimmy's wasn't pierced.

"Okay, let me check on Dean and we'll all sit down for dinner."

"Just show me where the plates and silverware are and I'll get the tables set," Rage said. He really was a good guy.

"I'll help you," Janelle said, coming around from Jimmy's area.

I noticed Henry checking her out. The second this storm was over, I was firing him.

"I'll help, too," Oliver said, and I realized he'd seen Henry's leering look as well.

I knew Janelle had Jimmy there, but it still made me feel better leaving her with a couple more bodyguards.

Dean insisted he was feeling fine, and I insisted he come down and eat with us, then. He sighed. "I walked right into that one, didn't I?"

"Yes, you did. You're not leaving me alone with all those people. I feel like tension is getting higher and people are getting drunker."

When we got back downstairs, I nearly ran into Henry, who was hovering in the doorway, texting. The guy definitely loved his phone. Inside the pub, the food was all laid out on the tables that had been pushed together and there seemed to be some maneuvering for seats. Dave nearly tripped over his own feet trying to land the spot next to Madeline, and Bryce and the woman with him seemed to be eager to be at the very end of the table. I took the chair next to the woman.

"I'm sorry," I said. "I don't know your name. I'm Sophie, if I didn't already mention that. I'm the owner."

"I know who you are," she said.

Taken aback, I wasn't sure what to make of that. "Great, then. Your name?" I prompted again. I couldn't eat dinner next to someone whose name I didn't know.

"Lillian," she finally said, before shoving a piece of cornbread in her mouth.

Suddenly I knew why she looked familiar. "Oh my gosh, you're Mimi Sinclair's personal assistant!"

Mimi Sinclair was an It Girl a decade earlier when we had all been in our teens. She'd been twenty-five, with an ego as big as her booming career. Lillian had been in hundreds of shots posted on social media with Mimi, holding her handbag, balancing an umbrella over her, carrying her chihuahua, and scrambling ahead to open doors for her.

"Used to be," she said, over a mouthful of bread. She chewed hard, swallowed, and looked generally miserable.

Just like she had in all those photos.

"What do you do now?" I asked, reaching for a potato and dropping it on my plate. Hopefully Lillian had moved on to greener pastures. She had certainly seemed celebratory when she was drinking her champagne earlier. Her mood now seemed an about-face.

"She's my assistant," Bryce said, not allowing Lillian to answer for herself. "And my girlfriend."

I stared at Bryce, struggling to be polite. He was such a jerk. Lillian had gone from one egomaniac to another. "What work do you do, then?" I asked, determined to make Bryce cough up the truth behind what he was doing in Friendship Harbor. These were not ski tourists.

"I'm a consultant."

The only thing I would consult with him on was how to be a jerk.

Wait a minute. Pulling my phone out of my back pocket I set it in my lap and tried to discreetly type in Bryce Holden's name. It popped up immediately and I knew exactly what Bryce was doing.

"You work for Hollywood Has Beens!" I gasped, outraged. "That stupid horrible show that spies on former child stars and actors who have left the business."

The table erupted.

"What?" Brett yelled, standing up so fast his chair fell backward. "Is this loser calling me a has-been?"

I wasn't sure why Brett thought this was about him, specifically. I suspected he was calling all of us has-beens. Or me, for sure, anyway.

Bryce stood up just as fast, but instead of posturing at Brett, he turned and ran across the pub.

"What is he doing?" Dave asked.

"He's getting his laptop," Lillian murmured so low I just caught it.

"Grab his laptop!" I yelled to the room at large.

Madeline screamed, though I wasn't sure why.

George stuck his boot out and tripped Bryce, who sprawled across the wooden pub floor with a loud thud. George went back to his chili.

Rage ran to the table where Bryce and Lillian had been camped out all day. He grabbed both laptops and brought them to Lillian. Bryce was scrambling to get off the floor. He lunged at Rage's back, but he was thinner and older and just bounced off of the muscular actor.

"Do that again and I'm going to have to restrain you," Dean said, also standing up. "Or we'll lock you in the office."

"Show me what you sent back to your people," Rage said, handing Lillian the laptops.

"No!" Bryce said.

Lillian didn't hesitate. "It already aired, so I might as well show them, Bryce. It would take them five seconds to find it. It was even on TV briefly when someone was channel surfing earlier."

She opened her laptop, typed quickly, then turned it to face all of us sitting at the table.

The Ski Trip From Hell.

"Well, this is solid reporting so far," Oliver said, though his joke sounded more strained than genuine.

The entertainment reporter was standing in front of her big screen, which flashed a picture of everyone in the pub earlier, before Sienna had been found.

"On Wednesday's episode of Hollywood Has Beens, we're checking in on the gang from *The Hijinks of Haley and Jake*, who in addition to beginning taping the show, have been traveling together. In designer clothes and flashing cash in first Ibiza, the New York City, and now, Maine? It's true. It seems that all the current cast are in a remote town in Maine skiing and staying with Sophie LaFleur, who starred in the short-lived show *Murder, She Texted*."

A picture of me with Jack winning Blueberry King replaced the picture of everyone sitting around the pub in ski clothes.

"After her acting career ended, Sophie has spent the majority of her time showing farm animals in fairs."

That was absurd. And not even true. I'd been running a pub. Or assisting Dean in running the pub. I tried not to be offended and failed.

"But now she's gotten all her Hijinks friends into a *hairy* situation. Due to a big nor' Easter, they are all trapped in a pub by the name of Steamy's. That's ironic given the numerous romantic hookups rumored to be happening among the actors and the staff." A rapid montage of Sienna leaning into Rage appeared, then it flashed to Rage and Madeline, clearly in a heated discussion, and finally to Madeline in the corner of the pub with...Henry? "Should make for interesting days on the set, right?" The reporter gave a big grin.

I couldn't believe this was happening. I had spent all day being friendly and solicitous to Bryce and Lillian and they were trying to make me and my friends look bad.

"Catch the whole episode on Wednesday." The chipper reporter's face changed as she clearly read something on the teleprompter. "On a somber note to this same story, it's now been reported to our team here at HHB that Sienna Lawrence, who was to play the role of Haley in the revitalized series, has been found dead on Sophie LaFleur's property. There is no official cause of death to report at this time given the current state of snow emergency in Maine, but it is believed to be from a drug overdose. Wow, this is such shocking news. Our condolences to the many family and friends of Sienna. Again, we just learned that Sienna Lawrence is dead at the age of twenty-seven."

Sienna's headshot popped up on the screen and we all sat there, stunned. Seeing Sienna's picture and having her death reported publicly made it feel as stark and real as discovering her body had.

"You son of a—" Oliver leaped out of his chair and grabbed Bryce by the shirt. He shook him. "How could you do that to Sienna? You're a disgusting piece of trash."

I had never once seen Oliver violent, so I jumped up too. "Oliver!" I was afraid he would get injured if he tried to take a swing at Bryce.

"Give me your phones and the laptops," Dean said, sounding grim. "No more sending pictures or information until we're all out of here. Sienna's family didn't even know she is gone and now they're going to find out from a stupid TV sound bite."

Lillian, looking chastened, actually handed her cell phone over readily to Dean and gave him the two laptops. Bryce had shaken off Oliver and was holding his hands up as Rage stood in front of him, hands clenched in fists.

"I'm not giving you my phone," Bryce said.

"You don't have a choice," Rage said. He reached out and yanked Bryce's phone away from him and put it in his pocket.

Brandy was sitting there calmly, eating her dinner. Madeline was chewing her bottom lip, clearly upset. Jimmy and Janelle were eating too, looking unconcerned with the dust-up. George still sat at the bar. He took a sip of his beer. I guess what they said about Mainers was true. It was hard to rattled them.

"Where's Henry?" I asked, realizing the dishwasher was missing. Again. "Why isn't he eating?"

"He's probably in the kitchen," Janelle said. "I wouldn't worry about it."

She definitely didn't sound concerned.

"Why don't I lock all the electronics in the safe in the office?" Dean said. "I think we all need some reassurance that private conversations aren't being broadcast online." He and Rage both moved in the direction of the office. I followed, deciding to use that moment to check on Jack. I needed a minute to clear my head from all of this drama.

Unfortunately, Jack seemed to be having some drama himself. As soon as we stepped in the office, I could hear him kicking up a fuss in the hallway. I wondered if he needed a potty break outside. I wasn't sure I could go back out there in the snow but a llama mama's work is never done. And the cold air might actually do me some good.

"Hey, buddy," I said, rubbing his neck. "Let's do this really quick, okay?" I led him to the back door. Grabbing one of Grammy's coats and hats, I bundled up and stuck my feet in her boots that were a tad too small for me. I shoved the door open and was immediately hit by a blast of cold air. Snow pelted me in the face, and I could barely see five feet in front of me, the wind swirling the flakes in circles.

"You have to be fast," I repeated to Jack, taking two feet outside onto my front porch. It wasn't an ideal spot, but this was desperate times. It was so cold it hurt my lungs to breathe. I kept opening my mouth and making little "uhh" sounds, like that was going to make it less cold.

Jack seemed to have self-preservation on his mind. Being right out in the elements was a far cry from his hay-filled shed. He did his thing and looked at me like "let's get out of here."

"Good boy," I said. "Such a good boy!" I stepped back into the hallway and slammed the door shut behind me. I whimpered a little, shoulders stiff, fingers numb. My hair that was outside of the knit hat was wet from the snow. "This is bananas," I told Jack.

He snorted and bobbed his head up and down. I took it as a nod of agreement.

I settled him back into the hallway and took the coat and boots off. I left the hat on. I was chilled to the bone. I could use some hot cocoa. Or maybe to actually eat the chili I hadn't gotten to enjoy because of Bryce Holden.

Madeline was pacing in front of the kitchen, her phone constantly dinging with notifications. "This is my mother," she announced. "She's freaking out. Someone told her about Sienna." She studied the screen. "I need to call her and my phone is about to die. My charger's in the office." Then she just headed to the office without waiting for a response from anyone.

For a moment, I thought about the phones and laptops. But they were locked up, and I had no idea why she would want access to them anyway. Dean and Rage were already back at the table. Dean was eating. Rage was fuming.

"Is Henry still missing?" I asked Brandy as I picked up my bowl of chili from the table. I needed to reheat it.

"I guess." She shrugged. "Hey, Soph?"

"Yes?"

"Do you think Oliver's right? That the silver fox is just being polite to me?" She looked like it was all she'd thought about the last few hours. Not about the snowstorm or Sienna. Or the fact I was being touted as a fair-going, country girl. Which I kind of was, but still.

I sighed. "I don't know. But he doesn't live here anyway. Maybe he's not really the right fit for you."

She frowned, but she didn't say anything. She just went back to clearing the dishes from the table. "I'm not washing these," she snapped. "Henry needs to earn his paycheck."

"I agree."

"Sophie?" George asked, approaching the table. "What's your

friend's name, the skinny kid who has a very high opinion of himself?"

"Brett?" Unless he meant Oliver. It could be a toss-up.

"Yeah, sure," George said. "I think he's dead in the corner."

"What?" I gasped. George sounded remarkably calm. He was a total Mainer. "Where?"

Please let it be Brett and not Oliver. Then I felt terrible for my selfish and unkind thought. *But please don't let it be Oliver.*

Then I realized Oliver was sitting at the bar next to Dean, very much alive.

George pointed to the poorly lit back left corner. I could see Brett slumped over on the floor. Running over there, I slowed down at the last minute, not wanting to touch him and find him cold. He looked like he'd sat down, legs out, back against the wall, then had died. His head was lolling forward, but there were no signs of injury.

I basically tiptoed toward him, heart racing.

"Is he dead?" George said, right behind me.

I jumped. I didn't realize he was that close to me. "Why don't you check?" I asked.

"He ain't my friend."

Glaring at George, I bent down tentatively. Right then Brett started snoring. "Oh thank goodness, he's alive." I peered closer. He reeked like liquor. "I think he's just drunk."

Which frankly, George should have recognized. He was well-acquainted with alcohol himself.

"My mistake." George wandered away. He swiped a piece of cornbread out of the bowl on the table.

I grabbed my chest, taking a deep breath. I couldn't take another scare. "Brett, are you okay?" I asked, giving him a little shake. "I can get you a blanket."

He mumbled something under his breath and waved his hand, like he was trying to push me away. Fine. He was on his own. He was going to have wicked neck pain the next day. Though part of me envied him being asleep right now. I wouldn't mind closing my eyes and waking up tomorrow to find this was all a bad dream.

Madeline came back into the pub, smiling and holding a bag of gummy worms. "Look what I found in my bag!" she said. "I forgot I had these stashed."

She sounded like a ten-year-old. I wasn't even sure what to say to her at this point. "Did you get to talk to your mom?" I asked her.

"Huh?" For a flash, she gave me a blank stare. "Oh, yes, totally. She was relieved but so scared for me. It's basically like we're cut off from the world here. I told her it's fine."

"It is fine," I reassured her. Though that was debatable.

Finally getting back to my chili, I reheated it and took a seat at the bar, where everyone but Bryce and Lillian had gathered. I wasn't sure if it was the TV or the sense of normalcy, but the bar was a gravitational force. I was just tucking into my chili when George started speaking.

"It was a night just like tonight," George said, nursing a beer from his regular stool. He appeared to have settled into his favorite spot to ride out the rest of this horrible storm. "The night that everything changed. None of us were ever the same."

"What?" I asked him, startled by his ominous tone. George generally wasn't one to sound so melodramatic. If he was going to tell some kind of urban legend to scare us, I was going to lose it. This wasn't camp.

George turned and looked at us, lifting his beer to his mouth and taking a deep swallow. "We were in the woods, a dozen of us, caught off guard by a snowstorm that had the wind howling so hard a man couldn't hear the thoughts in his head. Do you know what that kind of cold feels like? Knives buried into your flesh, that's what it feels like. And you can't breathe because the air scrapes your lungs and holds you hostage."

I could attest to that from my two minutes outside with Jack.

"There was no shelter, just a couple of tarps we fashioned together after the crash."

The crash? My eyebrows rose.

"George, we've heard this story," Dean said, dryly.

"Shh," I said. I wanted to hear it. "Go ahead, George."

He didn't need much encouragement. "We were dang near frozen to death, down to our last emergency flare, with the sinking feeling that no one was coming for us, which they weren't. Then they showed up. We sensed it first, something out there. The realization that we weren't alone, and it wasn't man coming for us, but beast. Out of the deep bowels of the inky dark nighttime forest, they emerged, one right after the other, circling us, judging size and weakness and who they might be able to pick off first."

"Oh, dear," Madeline said, taking a seat next to me, bag of gummies still in her hand.

Everyone had gotten quiet to listen to George's monologue, even Dean, though he did give a sigh of exasperation here and there. The lights in the pub momentarily flickered, causing Madeline to reach for my arm as she gave a startled gasp. I breathed easier when the power remained on.

"Time slowed down, just briefly. We all stood there, listening, knowing, sending up a prayer and wishing we could see our loved ones one more time. Then there was nothing but screams, then silence. Silence, then screams, as they tore through our makeshift camp and went for the kill. A man learned a lot about himself that night. None of it good."

Um... I looked to Dave for help. "What's he talking about?" If we were about to be descended into a Stephen King novel, I had a real problem with that.

"Martens. A furbearing member of the weasel family with partially retractable claws. George's camp got attacked by a marten gang."

I had no idea what to say to that. But George had clearly survived to tell the tale.

"They can take down a whole deer," George said.

The gummy worm Madeline had been chewing on fell to the bar. "Oh, dear," she repeated.

"I don't think they call it a gang," Brandy said.

"Dave is right. This was a gang, I tell you," George insisted. "And it was an organized attack. Those vicious vermin planned to pick us off, one by one."

"Did anyone get killed?" I asked, just to reassure myself. I had a feeling the answer was no, but I needed to know.

"No one got killed," Brandy said. "George is exaggerating."

"What do you know, whippersnapper? Were you there? Did you look into the eyes of the devil? Because I did." George lifted his beer. "Why do you think I drink?"

Brandy snorted.

"No one was killed," Dave reassured me. "But Hatchet Spears had his fingernail ripped off when he was running away."

I was trying to process that, when the lights went out. The pub was plunged into darkness, and someone screamed. I was pretty sure it was Madeline.

It definitely wasn't Brandy because she yelled, "Zip it! Hollering doesn't help anything."

"No one move," Dean said. "I'll go turn on the generator."

A small light came on and I realized it was the flashlight on his phone. He got down off his stool, light bouncing around as he did.

Good plan. I pulled my own phone out of my pocket and turned on the flashlight right as Dean's light retreated. When my light came on, I realized Madeline was practically climbing up the length of Dave's body. He was awkwardly patting her back.

Good grief. I felt like I needed to warn Dave he was in over his head, but I reminded myself he was a big boy, albeit a naive one.

Something just occurred to me. "Wait. Is Hatchet Spears Pinky Spears' husband?" I'd only met Pinky this past Christmas. She was the seriously no-nonsense church secretary at the Methodist church. I was a little scared of her. So, it made sense she might have a husband named Hatchet.

"Yep," Janelle said, wandering around behind the bar looking for something. She kept bending down and feeling around with her hands in the dark.

"I'm just going to assume Hatchet and Pinky are nicknames."

"Hatchet is. Pinky is her given name."

I wasn't about to ask how he'd earned the nickname Hatchet. Or why on earth a couple looked at one another and decided to name their newborn Pinky.

"What are you looking for?" I asked. "Here, take my phone to use the flashlight."

"My phone. I left it behind the bar before and now I can't find it."

"Does Jimmy have it?"

She gave a tinkling laugh. "Do you know my grandfather at all? He still has a flip phone that he barely even uses. He would not take my phone."

The California crew had no need to steal a phone. "Maybe someone thought it was theirs."

"It will turn up." She handed me my phone back. "Thanks."

Janelle didn't sound too concerned, so I wasn't going to worry about it.

I had enough to worry about. Thanks to Bryce, I had a feeling once the storm was over, I was going to find the pub invaded by reporters. Or at least curiosity seekers.

The lights came back on, though feebly.

Phew.

Madeline peeled herself off of Dave.

That was at least an improvement. I ate my chili and mulled over Sienna's death. Madeline's behavior. Something was not right here and I was going to figure it out.

The brief respite disappeared. The room went dark again.

EIGHT

DEAN REAPPEARED a minute later and sat down next to me. The lights had flickered on again.

I leaned close to Dean and whispered, "Should the light still be flickering while they are running on the generator?"

"Well, no. But that also depends on how much propane we have left."

Great, I wasn't thrilled about the idea of continually sitting around in the dark with this group of people. Thanks to that charming little piece that Bryce had done on everyone, me included, and spilling the news of Sienna's death, the tension in the room was nearly as thick as the snow. And we still had Henry lurking around somewhere. Definitely not the type of guy who I wanted to be stuck with in a dark room. The super creeper.

"With any luck the generator will keep running long enough for the lights to come back on," Dean said, clearly trying to reassure me. I appreciated the effort, but I think we both knew the likelihood of that happening was pretty much zero to none. With all the heavy snow and wind, the chances of the electrical crews getting all the power back might be a couple days. And let's face it, by then, this group would be freezing to death and possibly eating their own.

"I hate this," Madeline said.

She'd been a wreck since the lights had gone out, and frankly, it was starting to get on my nerves. It wasn't as if any of us were having the time of our lives here. I was supposed to be headed to a bed-and-breakfast with Dean tomorrow. Now, I was stuck in a pub with a group of upset actors, a weird dishwasher, a drunk guy passed out in the corner and after that marten story, I was even having my doubts about George Sprague.

From the corner, Brett snorted, mumbled a few unintelligible words and went back to snoring.

"Maybe we could play a game or something," Dave suggested from where he sat on the bar.

"What kind of game?" I said, eager for something to change the vibe of the room.

"Well, you guys already played twenty questions with me. So, if that is the suggestion, I think I will sit out," Bryce grumbled, strolling up to the bar like he wasn't the world's biggest jerk. Everyone shot him a dirty look.

Seriously, how was he the injured party here? He was the one making money off of their misfortune. I was still irritated that he'd made the piece. Sophie LaFleur showing farm animals 24/7. Sure, I'd left acting, but seriously?

"I can't believe you are the one upset," Oliver said, voicing my very thoughts. "You made us look like pretentious idiots."

The depiction of their behavior wasn't totally inaccurate, but I wasn't going to say that. And really, the piece did make everyone look their worst. Except for Jack. He'd looked quite regal in his Blueberry King crown. And couldn't they have at least shown my hot boyfriend?

Okay, I really needed to let this go.

"I did you all a favor," Bryce said, doing a fair job of being pretentious himself. "Haven't you heard all exposure is good exposure? It's not like *The Hijinks of Haley and Jake* is likely to be a go now. I'd say my piece ended up being a perfectly timed bit of exposure. I mean, you could still get jobs from it."

Madeline turned to Rage, her eyes huge. "Wait, the reboot isn't going to happen?"

Rage looked amazed that the thought hadn't occurred to her before this. "I mean, it might. But we did just lose the actress playing one of the main characters in the cast."

She gaped at him, then around to all of us. "I don't get it. We still have Oliver. We have me. We even have Brett back. Okay, so Sienna was taking over the role of Haley but she wasn't that fabulous an actress. I'm sure the producers could still recast her."

I blinked, stunned at her callousness. Everyone sported some version of the same expression. Even Jimmy cocked a surprised eyebrow.

"I don't think we should talk about this right now," Rage said calmly.

Madeline turned in her barstool to stare at him. "This is your fault, do you know that?"

Rage's fault? Clearly, everything was getting to her. They said cabin fever was a real thing. Could the insanity hit in just eight hours? Then again, normally cabin fever wasn't accompanied by death.

Rage said nothing. Brandy poured him a glass of wine. Madeline slumped on her stool, glaring off into space.

Yeah, this night was really deteriorating. Quickly.

"So, what game were you thinking of, Dave?" I asked, trying to save what I could.

Dave stared down at the beer in his hand. I got the feeling his Madeline worship had just died a sudden death.

He lifted his head and cleared his throat. "We could play charades."

"Great idea," I said, standing up. The lack of excitement from the others was inescapable, but I clapped my hands and managed my best perky cruise director persona. "Come on. This will be fun."

Oliver stood too. "I'm in."

I appreciated his solidarity.

"Me too," Brandy said from behind the bar. She paused to pour herself a large glass of wine before she came out to the pub floor to join me and Oliver. She paused and grabbed the whole bottle. I couldn't begrudge her needing more than a little bit of liquid enthusiasm.

Though we were going to need to call our distributor and order more alcohol after this storm. The bottles were going down quickly.

"Okay, so Oliver, Brandy, and I will be the team captains, and we'll just do an old-fashioned schoolyard pick, okay?"

Nobody responded, except for Jimmy who chose that moment to head back into the kitchen.

"Alright," I said with a smile. "Oliver, why don't you pick first."

"I pick Dean," he said without hesitation. He smirked at me.

Really? "I'm wounded."

Dean nodded. "Good choice. I'm a charades master."

I laughed, trying to get into the spirit. "Dave, this was a great idea. Let me think about my pick." I tapped my finger against my pursed lips as I considered. "Rage, come on over to Team Victory."

He needed a little boost after being yelled at by Madeline. He didn't look thrilled, but he pushed up out of his chair and joined me.

Brandy went next, picking Dave, who still looked like he found out the Easter Bunny wasn't real. Poor guy.

Madeline still scowled into space as if none of us were there.

"I'm going to go with guy power," Oliver announced. "I choose George."

George nodded as if to say Oliver had clearly made another wise and strategic move. He adjusted his John Deere hat and joined Team Oliver.

"I have to go with my girl, Janelle." I waved her over, and she jogged across to me, waving her hands in the air like she'd just won on a game show.

Brandy glanced at Madeline, who rose and went to sit at a table by the window, staring out at the snow. Brandy made a "whatever" face and pointed to Lillian.

"Oh wow, what a surprise. I'm the last one picked. Who would have guessed that," Bryce said.

"Actually, I think we should make you a floater," I suggested. "Since the teams will be uneven if you join one, you can just jump in and help each team."

He shrugged as if it made no different to him if he played or not. But I had a sneaking suspicion he was happy to be included. After all, what was the quote? "Be somebody who makes everybody feel like somebody." Even if said somebody referred to you as a has-been.

"Alright, Dave, what's next?" I asked.

"We need to make up some slips of paper with things to act out on them."

"Okay. We can use our order pads and everybody can write up--let's say five things each to act out." We might as well make a bunch of them considering we had a long night ahead of us. Dave spun on top of the bar and jumped down to retrieve the order pads and a handful of pens. He came back over the top of the bar and brought them to the group table.

"Everybody think of some great ideas," I said encouragingly as we all settled in around the table.

The lights flickered again, and I looked up at the lights. Not now. We actually had everybody in a somewhat good place. With the exception of Madeline, who seemed determined to be a grump. I refocused on my pad, writing down Jack the llama, because, hey, why wouldn't I? I just finished folding the paper when I noticed the lights seemed to be dimming. We all looked around us as the light faded more and more until we were in the pitch dark.

"Awesome," someone said. I was pretty sure it was Bryce.

Soon, several cell phone flashlights came on, the bright beams darting around and illuminating our faces in harsh, eerie light.

"Is everyone good?" Dean asked. I appreciated that at times like this, he was that steady, take-charge kind of guy. "It looks like the generator has run out of juice, so we're going to have to figure out a different light source. Everyone should try to keep their cell phones as charged as possible just in case we need them for emergencies."

Janelle stood up. "I think there is a new box of the tea candles that we use for the tables in the stockroom." She headed in that direction.

Madeline, who must have been frightened by the darkness, appeared, and headed straight to Rage. She hugged his arm, leaning her head against his shoulder. Rage leaned in to kiss her temple. I guess their tiff was over. Which was a good thing. No negativity, especially since we had a long, cold dark night ahead.

"I think we should still finish our words and phrases for char—" My sentence was cut off by a piercing shriek. Then another.

I immediately ran for the stockroom, knowing it had to be Janelle. The lights of several cell phones lit up her terrified features, giving the whole scene a Blair Witch quality. She screamed again.

"What is it?" I asked.

There was no explanation. She just continued screaming at the top of her lungs. A figure moved past me and a palm whacked across Janelle's face. She blinked, confused.

"Sorry," Dave said from beside me.

I blinked too, realizing he'd been the one to slap Janelle. Peaceful, hippie, I-love-you, you-love-me Dave. Wow. Clearly, this night was taking its toll on everyone.

"Janelle, are you okay?" Dean asked.

She nodded, then shook her head. She was obviously in shock.

"What happened?" I asked.

She blinked, then finally pointed at the floor. All the cell phone lights moved in unison to where she gestured.

On the floor in the stockroom, sprawled facedown was Henry, an industrial-sized food can beside him. I thought it might be stewed tomatoes.

"Is he dead?" Brandy whispered, as if she didn't want to let him know he might be. "That looks like blood."

"Maybe that's tomato juice," I said. "From the can." Hopefully. There was an odd tinny odor in the air.

Dean crouched down next to him and pressed his fingers to Henry's neck. "I don't feel a pulse."

Great.

Everyone stood there for a moment. From the hallway, I heard some muffled pounding. Jack. Or at least I hoped it was Jack.

Dean rose and located the box of candles that Janelle had gone in there to get. He handed them out to Dave. "Everyone go out to the pub and get these lit."

Brandy put an arm around Janelle and led her past the others and out of the room. After a bit more shuffling, everyone followed. Just Dean and I were left in the stock room.

"Are you sure he's dead?" I felt like I had to ask again.

"Yeah. He's definitely not breathing and there is a lot of blood."

I missed that, probably because of the moving lightshow of cell phone flashlights. I cast my own phone light on Henry's body. Oh yeah, there was blood. Yikes.

This was unbelievable. "Should I call Justin again?"

Dean shook his head. "No, I'll give him a call. I think you should go back out there and try to keep everybody calm."

I felt pretty certain the game night option was off the table after this. But I nodded. Instead of going toward the pub, I turned in the direction of the office.

"Where are you going?"

"Don't you hear that?" There was another distant thud. "I know you don't want Jack in the pub, but I'm not leaving him out in the hall by himself. He doesn't like all this death."

"I'm pretty sure none of us like all the death," he pointed out. "But do you really think Jack even knows someone died?"

"When are you going to realize that Jack is very attuned to these things?"

I could tell Dean didn't believe me, but instead of debating, he just shooed me toward the office. "Fine, but I'm going with you. And this is only for tonight."

I smiled as I held my cell phone up to light the way. Even though I knew Dean would never admit it, I think he actually had a soft spot for Jack.

As soon as we opened the door to the hallway, Jack peeked out at us. His lips curled back over his two large front teeth.

"Oh, big guy," I said sympathetically. "Were you scared stuck here in the dark?"

"He sleeps in a dark barn every night."

I shot a disapproving frown at Dean, as I cuddled Jack's neck. I was pretty sure since I was holding the light, he couldn't see it, but I knew he could feel it.

"This isn't his barn though, is it? And you saw his scared little face." I snuggled Jack a bit more, before reaching for his lead.

"I thought you were worried about him being nervous about all the death and what not. Not scared of the dark."

"You don't want him to be scared or nervous, do you?"

He made a face that said he wasn't particularly worried about either problem, but he didn't say it. For which I was glad. Jack didn't like negativity any more than I did. Besides, I needed the comfort just as much as Jack did.

One death was explainable. Two was a crime spree.

Henry wasn't my favorite person in the world, but I didn't wish him dead. "Do you think that can just fell on his head?" I asked Dean.

"I don't know. I guess it's possible." Dean didn't sound convinced. "We don't even store the big cans and jars on the top shelves anymore, because Dave dropped a giant jar of maraschino cherries on his head last year. It was a sticky mess, but clearly it didn't kill him, so I have to assume this was a malicious attack."

I couldn't argue any of that. I lifted my phone light around the hallway just to be sure nothing was amiss. Jack's blanket was crumpled in the middle of the hallway floor, and there was hay strewn everywhere. But that looked like Jack could have done it simply by pacing around. And otherwise nothing looked unusual.

"Okay, let's get out of here." I pulled Jack's leash and he followed willingly.

Halfway through the office, Jack stopped. I turned, expecting to see him inspecting the cord he'd been interested in the last time we walked through the office. Instead he was nudging a small bottle that lay on the floor near a bag that had tipped over, some other contents spilled on the floor.

"Is everything okay?" Dean asked when he realized we'd stopped.

"Yeah, Jack is just being nosy."

"Who could he have learned that from?"

I made a face, although I was not sure he could see me. I quickly moved in and plucked the bottle away from Jack, inspecting the label. It was eye drops, and the bottle was empty.

It must have fallen out of the bag. I shoved the other items, a brush, a wallet, and a lip balm back in the bag, tossing the empty bottle on top. I gently pulled his lead and he started following again.

When we reached the stockroom, Jack stopped again, raising his snout in the air. He made a noise and his ears pitched forward.

I gave Dean an "I told you so" look. "See, he knows."

"I never claimed that animals weren't aware of death. I just don't think he was in the hallway freaking out because Henry got clocked on the head with a can of tomatoes. If that's what happened. But I don't see how a falling can could have enough force to kill him. A bump on the head, sure. But it would have only fallen a foot or two at most."

"What a way to go." Still stuck on the choice of weapon. "Death by stewed tomatoes. Even a jar of cling peaches or a large can of green beans would be better."

Dean nodded, although I got the distinct feeling he wasn't quite sure how to respond.

My observation was a little cold, I realized. You know, after I said it aloud. They said nurses and doctors developed a morbid sense of humor to cope with all the terrible things they saw around them. I was starting to think maybe I was developing one, too. That, in and of itself, was a little sobering.

He must have seen my regret, because he gave me a quick kiss. "Go ahead and get Jack situated. I'm going to call Justin."

After a few more tugs, I got Jack through the stockroom and into the pub. The whole room was aglow with dozens of candles. It reminded me of some eerie castle or church from a horror movie.

Dave was behind the bar, pouring beer, which he then placed in front of George. He poured another and placed it in front of Oliver. Bryce and Lillian were seated back at pushed-together tables, still keeping their distances from the rest of the group. Rage also sat at the bar, while Madeline paced up and down the length of the room, chewing on the nail of her index finger.

"Where's Janelle? Is she okay?" I asked.

"Yeah, she's in the kitchen with Jimmy," Brandy said from where she was lighting and setting out more candles on the empty tables.

I looked around, trying to decide where I could put Jack. The stockroom was out, and making a pen with chairs wouldn't work. He could just push them aside and then break free, and frankly, I was too sore from all my outdoor activities to wrestle with any more heavy tables. So, I just dropped his lead. Roam free, my friend. I'd worry about any mess he made tomorrow.

"You can't just let that thing go," Madeline said, stopping her pacing.

"He won't hurt anything," Dave said defensively. The crush was definitely gone. "Jack Kerouac is a class act."

George laughed. "That sort of rhymes. I like that."

Jack just remained standing near the stockroom door, staring at everyone. Probably wondering why they were all staring at him. Or wondering how he ended up at this dud party.

"He really is harmless," I assured everyone. I was not going to mention that he might spit if he decided he wasn't a fan.

Madeline began pacing again.

Rage shifted on his barstool and caught her arm as she made another swing past him. "Will you sit down? You're just making everyone crazy. And if you are worried about the llama, I think just keeping still would be wise."

Madeline shot a worried look at Jack. He chose that moment to take a couple steps farther into the room. She let out a little squeak and scrambled onto the stool between Rage and Oliver.

Oliver grimaced at her, clearly not wanting her neuroses near him. He took his beer and headed over to snag a piece of cornbread off the table. He brought it to Jack and offered it to him.

Jack accepted gladly, doing his happy lip-smacking, side-to-side chewing.

"See, he's super adorbs," Oliver said, petting his pal's wooly neck and taking a sip of his beer. Jack already loved Oliver, but cornbread definitely sweetened the deal.

"I cannot believe we are going to have to spend the night with yet another dead body and a llama," Bryce said, rolling his eyes. He put his feet up on the empty chair next to him, leaning back, looking thoroughly disgusted.

"It's not the worst thing you've done to get a story," Lillian snapped.

Yikes. Things were getting ugly with those two. I guess snowstorms and possible murder got things real, real fast.

"Can you watch Jack for me?" I asked Oliver. "I want to check on Janelle."

"Sure. I haven't spent much time with my favorite, two-hundred-pound, fuzzy pet. And I'm sorry I haven't spent much time with my very best friend either." He smiled regretfully.

I gave him a hug. I appreciated that he realized that. "You had me at favorite, two-hundred-pound, fuzzy pet."

He laughed as he returned my hug. "I got too caught up in the whole idea of having my acting career back."

"I get that," I said, pulling back to look at him. "I'd probably have been just as wrapped up in the whole thing, if the tables were turned."

He smiled a little sadly. "No, you wouldn't. And we both know it, but thank you for trying to make me feel like less of an awful friend."

I gave him another quick hug. "Don't let Jack eat any chili. We do not want that additional disaster tonight." I was only half joking.

Oliver grimaced. "Not a problem."

Going into the kitchen, I saw my cook awkwardly patting his granddaughter on the back. He gave me a grimace over her shoulder. Again, I saw the family resemblance. As much as a crusty old man can resemble a pixie-like twentysomething woman.

"Janelle, are you okay?"

She nodded, and stepped back from Jimmy. "It was just a shock. That was a lot of blood. I don't like blood."

"That's understandable."

"I think I'm just going to stay in here with Jimmy," Janelle said, curling up in the desk chair at the small desk where Jimmy did his ordering and inventory.

It made me feel a little less clueless hearing she used his first name to refer to him.

Jimmy retrieved his thick, down parka from a hook near the back door and draped it over her. She let her head rest on the back of the chair and closed her eyes.

"Do you think she'll be okay?" I whispered. Janelle looked awfully pale.

"Ayuh."

It wasn't the best reassurance I'd ever gotten, but this was Jimmy we were talking about here. I had to trust him. His ancient radio played low in the background. Clearly, Jimmy had more forethought with his music than we'd had with our generator. The strains of Hotel California and the flicker of candles did make the kitchen feel more peaceful than the pub area. I kind of wanted to stay in here too.

But I couldn't do that.

"Let me know if you need anything."

Jimmy nodded. I think Janelle had already dozed off.

As soon as I stepped out of the kitchen, Lillian appeared in front of me.

I jumped, pressing a hand to my chest. "Jeezum crow," I gasped, utilizing one of my favorite Maine expletives. "You scared me."

"I'm sorry," she said, casting a look over her shoulder. "But I really need to talk to you. Alone."

Alone was a bit hard to come by. With Jimmy and Janelle in the kitchen that was out. Henry splayed on the stockroom floor, which made for a whole lot of eerie awkwardness. The only option was the restroom. I pointed in that direction, but she immediately shook her head.

"No, Bryce is in the bathroom right now." I wasn't sure why that mattered. It wasn't as if we were going to go in the men's room, but I allowed her to grab the sleeve of my sweatshirt and pull me off to the corner of the pub, near the stockroom.

Lillian glanced again at the restrooms, then quickly turned back to me. "Bryce went out to the barn and took pictures of Sienna's body," she said quietly.

I couldn't hide my shock. "Why would he do that?" Even though I was pretty sure I knew the answer.

"He plans to sell them to the highest bidder."

Yep, that was exactly what I expected her to say. He planned to sell them to some gossip rag or website and make a small fortune. Honestly, his plan was so ghoulish, I didn't know what to say. But that did explain why the blanket had been unwrapped from Sienna's body.

"He took them on his cell phone. I just wanted you to know, so you could delete them before we got the phones back."

"So, he hasn't done anything with them yet?"

She shook her head. "No, I convinced him to wait until I could edit them. I told him the better and cleaner the shots were, the more money we could make."

That had been quick thinking and seemed to prove she wasn't nearly the monster Bryce was. It was sad, she'd gone from one bad employment situation to an even worse one. And Bryce was also her boyfriend. She could do so much better on both counts.

"Actually, we've contacted the sheriff again. When he gets here, I'll make sure to give him the phones and the laptop." I half expected her to protest, but all she did was nod.

"I'm really sorry," she said, and I could tell from her expression and the remorse in her dark eyes that she was being honest. Not to mention, she didn't have to tell me anything about this.

"You've done a really good thing. I truly appreciate it." Not only for Sienna but also for her family and friends. They didn't deserve to see Sienna lying in a barn in Maine frozen to death—or however she died.

I expected Lillian to leave, hurrying back to the table before Bryce came out of the bathroom, but instead she glanced over her shoulder again, then back to me.

"Also..." She paused, uncertainty clear on her face. She bit her bottom lip, but then took a breath and blurted out her next admission. "Also, Bryce was the one who hit your friend and knocked him unconscious."

I stared at her for a moment. "Why?"

"When he was out there, sneaking the picture, he ran into Dean on the way back. He even admitted that he didn't think that he saw him, but he still picked up a branch and hit him over the head with it."

Holy llama, what a jerk. Dean could have been killed. There was clearly nothing that Bryce Holden wouldn't do to get the story. Or rather, make the big sale.

"Thank you," I said again.

She nodded and then left me to go back to her place where she had been sitting at the tables. A few moments later, Bryce came out of the bathroom.

I stood there, watching them and debating what to do. This was some seriously shady behavior. And criminal too. I needed to tell Dean so that he could tell Justin. I looked around the pub. Dean was nowhere to be found. He was probably still talking to Justin or maybe he was having a hard time reaching him.

I turned toward the dark stockroom. Was he still in there?

I tiptoed over, although I wasn't exactly sure why I felt the need to be so stealthy.

"Dean?" I listened. No answer. "Dean?"

I cautiously took a step into the room. I really did not want to be in here with Henry's corpse, although he was certainly less threatening in his current state than he was earlier. Poor Henry. Such a bad rap for having a creepy smile.

I pulled out my cell phone and turned on the flashlight and moved farther into the room.. Definitely no Dean. but I heard his voice coming from the office. I could tell, even from just his side of the conversation, he was talking to Justin.

I walked in the direction of the office, when my foot connected with something. It skittered across the wood floor. I shone my light onto the floor, at first seeing nothing. Then the beam glinted off of something under one of the metal rack shelves. I bent down to discover it was a cell phone. How on earth had we missed this before. Was it Janelle's? I picked it up and tapped the screen. A picture of a buxom pinup girl appeared on the homescreen. Well, I had no doubt this must have been Henry's.

"Okay, we'll see you when you can get here," I heard Dean say, his voice getting louder as he moved toward me. I quickly shoved Henry's phone in my back pocket.

"Wait, wait," I called out as Dean appeared in the doorway, but it was too late. Dean had already disconnected the call.

"What's wrong?" Dean said, not managing to keep the dread out of his voice. "Please don't tell me there's someone else dead."

"No," I said instantly as if that was the most ridiculous thing ever. But was it really? "No," I repeated reassuringly. "I just had an interesting talk with Lillian. She told me that Bryce was the one who knocked you unconscious."

"What?" Dean said, reflexively touching the bump on the back of his head. He dropped his hand and I half expected him to storm out to the pub to confront Bryce. Instead, he asked, "Why on earth would he do that?"

"Because he was out taking pictures of Sienna, which he plans to sell to the media, and you were out there, too, working on the generator. He was worried that you might spot him."

"Are you sure we can trust Lillian?"

I nodded. "I saw for myself that Bryce had been outside. His shoes and pants were wet and he even admitted he'd gone out—supposedly to try to get their car dug out."

"But isn't she his girlfriend? Why would she rat on him?"

"I think the guilt is getting to her. Selling death photos is really hard to stomach."

Dean considered that, then shook his head. "I tell you what, I can see why you left L.A."

NINE

"OKAY, the sheriff is on his way back here," Dean announced as we walked back into the pub. "He said we all stay together until he arrives."

"Does that mean we're all suspects?" George asked, sounding a little excited about the idea.

"Oh, I'm not sure we're *all* suspects," I said as I narrowed a suspicious look at Bryce, "but I think it's safer if we all stay together."

"This is ridiculous," Bryce said, rolling his eyes and leaning back in his chair. "This whole situation is turning into one of the horrible episodes of your TV show."

I glared at him. This jerk was really getting on my nerves. Photographing the dead body of my friend, assaulting my boyfriend, mocking my new lifestyle, and now badmouthing my somewhat popular TV show. Seriously.

"I think this will be a whole lot more pleasant if you just stayed quiet," Dean said to Bryce. I wasn't sure how Dean was restraining himself from punching Bryce right in the face.

Bryce rolled his eyes, but kept his mouth shut.

"My wife loved *Murder, She Texted*," George said.

"Thank you, George."

Speaking of my TV show, I remembered the phone in my back pocket.

"I have to use the ladies' room," I said, giving Brandy a pointed look. "Bran, will you go with me? I think it's fine if we go in pairs."

Brandy nodded, catching my prompt. "Sure."

"Actually, I have to go too," Oliver said.

"I can go with you," Rage offered.

Oliver waved a hand for him to stay put. "I'm sure the girls don't care if I go with them, right?" Obviously, he'd caught my look at Brandy, too. Great, I thought I'd been subtle, but now I wondered if others had noticed.

I smiled easily. "Sure, it wouldn't be the first time we've been in the ladies' room together. How many times have we done that in L.A. clubs?"

"Actually, you usually went in the men's room with me," Oliver said. He glanced back at the room. "The lines at ladies rooms are ridiculous."

The three of us stepped into the bathroom. I was pleased to see that someone, probably Brandy, had the foresight to put some of the tea candles around the bathroom. As soon as the door swung closed, I turned to my friends and I pulled the phone out of my back pocket.

"I found this on the floor near Henry. I think it's his phone," I said, keeping my voice just above a whisper. "Maybe there is something on here that might help us figure out what happened to him."

Both of them crowded around me.

Oliver snorted as the home screen lit up. "Of course he'd have a picture like that."

"Have you tried opening it yet?" Brandy asked.

"No." I tried swiping my finger across the screen. I fully expected to be prompted for a password, but the cell opened right up to the apps. I found the text message app and tapped it. A list of texts popped up. I just scrolled through.

"Whoa," Oliver said. "He texts more than I do."

I nodded. "He's always on his phone." I read through the snippets of texts that I could see without tapping on them. One thing became clear. "I think he was dealing drugs."

I tapped on one of the texts. "Yep, these are definitely messages about setting up sales." I tapped on another. More references to cost and where the person contacting Henry could meet him.

"That was what he was doing when he went outside all the time," Brandy said.

It was.

"He uses only initials or codes or something," Oliver pointed out. It was true, all the contacts were saved just by letters. JB, LN, CG. Every contact. Just letters.

I went back to the main list in his texts and tapped on the last texts he'd received. These were all sent by him to SRH.

Eye drops, huh? Sneaky, sneaky. Very deveous.

U better cough up the money. Soon

I will tell everyone what I saw. U better take this serious.

"He misspelled devious," Oliver pointed out.

"Eye drops? Is that code for drugs or something?" Brandy asked.

"Or can you put drugs in them?" I'd never heard of such a thing, but I didn't know much about drug other than my mother telling me to "just say no." Which I heeded.

"Drugs?"

We all started and gaped at the door. Madeline stood there, still holding the door open. She stepped inside.

"Who was dealing drugs? Whose phone is that?"

"It's Janelle's," I said. "I found it in the bathroom stall. She lost it."

Out of the corner of my eye, I saw Oliver nodding.

"You're going through it?" Madeline said. "That doesn't seem right."

"It's not," I agreed, pressing the button on the side of the phone. The screen went black.

"We shouldn't have," Brandy said. "But Janelle has been seeing a guy that we thought was bad news. And even though we knew we shouldn't have, we peeked at the texts from him."

"Did you find anything?"

I nodded. "It looks like he might have been dealing drugs."

"Might be," Oliver added quickly, covering for my use of past tense. "I bet he still is."

"Oh yeah, definitely," I said easily. "Yes, this guy is definitely too much of a bad boy for Janelle." I felt bad creating an awful love interest for sweet Janelle. She didn't even have a boyfriend, bad or otherwise. But letting anyone know we had Henry's phone was a bad idea. I'd definitely hand it over to Justin when he got here, but it couldn't hurt to see what we could find out about him before then.

Madeline studied us, then said, "Do you think this guy was around this week while we were here?"

Brandy nodded immediately. "I saw him stop by to see Janelle, I think on Tuesday or Wednesday." Clearly, we were all getting into our fictional story.

"So, maybe Sienna did buy some drugs from this guy," Madeline said. "I bet she was using again."

Oliver was shaking his head before Madeline even finished her theory. "I don't believe that for a minute. Sienna was way too excited about this new opportunity with the show. Plus, she told me just earlier today that she had reconnected with an old boyfriend. She was happy, and really thought it could work out this time. That just doesn't sound like somebody who would risk everything for some quick high on a vacation."

"She reconnected with an old boyfriend?" Madeline frowned. "She sure spent a lot of time flirting with other guys this week for someone who was really serious about someone from her past."

I have to admit I kind of agreed with that. She'd spent plenty of time checking out Dean since she'd been here. I also didn't doubt what George overheard Madeline and Rage fighting about. I didn't think for a minute that it wasn't beyond the realm of possibility that Sienna had made some kind of move on Rage.

"I just don't buy it," Oliver said, crossing his arms across his chest.

I hadn't really wanted to say anything about the items I found, but maybe it would prompt either Madeline or Oliver to remember something from this past week that they had forgotten or misinterpreted. So hesitantly, I said, "I did find some weird things in Sienna's suitcase and makeup bag."

"You were snooping in her stuff too?" Madeline said, appalled. "Sophie, I think you might have some sort of problem."

Others might agree with that, too.

Oliver frowned at me, his expression skeptical. "What kind of weird things did you see?"

"I found these rubber tubes in her suitcase and then in her makeup bag I saw something that looked like a syringe." I really hated having to bring it up since I knew toxicology was going to clarify everything anyway but it might reveal something. Obviously, Janelle's fictional boyfriend hadn't sold Sienna any drugs but from the texts, it looked like Henry could have. Of course, that didn't explain why Henry was now dead.

"Rubber tubes?" Oliver's frown deepened.

"They were rubber, or maybe silicone, and about ten or twelve inches long." I showed them the length with my hands. "I actually have one in my coat pocket."

Oliver stared at me, then made a face. "Those are sunglass bands. You attach them to the bows of our sunglasses to keep them on or around your neck. She had them to keep her glasses when she skied. And I guarantee you the syringe you found was tooth whitener. She'd complained to me that her teeth were yellowing, because of her love of lattes. I have the same problem, so I gave her a couple of the teeth whitening solutions that I got from my dentist. They come in prefilled syringes that you squeeze into a tray and wear for like twenty minutes. I even have a couple in my suitcase if you want to see whether they look the same."

Brandy, who'd not so subtly been inspecting his teeth as he talked, made an impressed face. "The whitener works great."

"Right?" Oliver said pleased, before turning his attention back to me to gauge my reaction.

"I have to admit that does make sense," I admitted. I had already been confused about why the tubes were neon colors, but if they were an accessory, that made total sense. And having the teeth whitener in her toiletry bag also made sense, too. "My mistake. Your teeth do look great," I added sheepishly.

Oliver shook his head, like he thought my sleuthing might have gotten out of hand. Which it might have.

"Okay, I really do have to go to the bathroom," I announced, then I realized that might sound as if I hadn't when I came in here. "I mean like really. I can't hold it anymore." I did a little desperate dance for good measure.

"Right," Brandy said. "Me too." She disappeared into the other stall.

"I hope you don't mind having to wait." I added through the door as I shoved Henry's phone in my front pocket.

"No problem," Madeline said. "You guys were in here first, right?"

After everyone used the bathroom—or at least attempted to, which was my case, we headed back out into the pub. Once again, the bar was the hangout spot. Even Jack, who was being watched by Dave and George. Only Bryce and Lillian still sat at the table, although they had moved closer to where everyone else was. I headed toward Dean when Madeline tapped me on the arm.

"Aren't you going to bring Janelle her phone? I know I feel completely lost without mine."

"Oh right." Of course, I'd had no intention of giving Janelle Henry's phone, but I headed in the direction of the kitchen, not wanting to cause any more questions. After a few steps, I realized Madeline was following me.

"Oh, I can go into the kitchen by myself. Both Janelle and Jimmy are in there, so I'll be fine," I said, assuming Madeline was going with me because of the announcement of the buddy system.

"Actually, I was hoping that I could find something sweet while

you are in there. When I'm stressed out, I crave sugar like crazy."
She giggled. "Do you mind? I don't want to go in there alone
anyway. Your silent cook kind of creeps me out."

Jimmy probably was the safest person here, but the fact he felt
no need to involve himself in unnecessary conversation was something that did take some time to get used to. I'd found it unnerving
at first, too.

"Sure, come on," I said, although I wasn't exactly thrilled with
the additional company. I couldn't figure out how to hand Janelle
the phone without her revealing it didn't belong to her. This was
not going to go well. Taking a deep breath, I push open the kitchen
door.

Janelle was still in the office chair at Jimmy's desk. She had
Jimmy's coat pulled up to cover her face and she was clearly asleep.
Jimmy was seated on a stool, his back against the wall and his arms
crossed over his chest. He appeared to be sleeping, too.

Madeline looked at Janelle and then to me as if waiting for me
to return the phone. I carefully placed it on the desk in front of
Janelle.

"I don't want to wake her. She was pretty shook up about
finding Henry," I whispered.

As soon as I got a chance, I would come back in and snag the
phone back. I knew there was more on Henry's phone that might
help us figure out, at least, what happened to him.

"Okay, so on our menu, we always have brownie sundaes,
cheesecake, and some kind of fruit cobbler. I think it's cherry
cobbler right now," I said softly, turning on the flashlight on my
phone.

"Oh, definitely brownie sundae," Madeline said with a grin.

I headed to the walk-in refrigerator, pausing for a moment with
my hand on the handle. The door would lock behind me if it were
to close. Did I really think Mads would actually consider locking
me in? And even if the door did shut, Jimmy and Janelle would
hear me if I banged on the door. Clearly, I'd seen too many movies
where somebody got stuck in one of these refrigerated rooms.

"I'll bring out the stuff to make them for everyone."

The temperature in the pub was going to continue to drop as long as we had no power, but we'd probably still lose a lot of our inventory. Maybe I should be focused on salvaging what I could of our food rather than snooping on Henry's phone. When it came to turning a decent profit here, we seemed to take one step forward, two steps back. We could put some of the food outside if necessary —although I wasn't sure what the health department would say about that method. I'd ask Dean what he thought.

Either way, it wasn't going to stay cold enough to keep the ice cream from melting. So an ice cream sundae party was a good plan. And maybe it would keep everyone somewhat entertained and together.

I unlatched the door and left the heavy steel wide open and hurried inside the refrigerated room. Still feeling nervous, I hurried to grab a sheet pan of Jimmy's homemade brownies and brought them back for Madeline to hold.

"I'll just get the ice cream."

I rushed back in to heft up a large tub of vanilla ice cream. Holy cow, it was seriously heavy. I placed my phone on top and grimaced as I held the freezing container with both arms against my chest. The bright light shining toward the ceiling made it difficult to see where I was going, and when I finally stumbled my way to the door, I noticed it was closed. What the heck?

"Madeline," I called, not hiding the panic in my voice.

The door immediately swung open.

"I'm sorry. Did I scare you?"

I stared at my friend, or at least what I could see of her through the blinding light. For a moment, I was certain I heard an eerie quality to her tone. Then she laughed, her usual almost childish giggle.

"I didn't mean to frighten you, I just figured you wanted to keep it as cold in there as you could."

Which was a reasonable conclusion. Did I really believe Madeline, who while sometimes annoying and high strung, would lock me in a walk-in? I was clearly feeling a little high strung myself. Although if Henry was killed, whoever did it was here among us. So, I suppose it was only wise to be a little bit suspicious of everyone.

"Okay," I said, adding a large container of chocolate syrup on top of the ice cream container. "Normally, we would have hot fudge but the hot fudge warmer has probably been off long enough that it's all congealed. So, syrup it is."

Madeline giggled. "Chocolate is chocolate, and it's all good."

Could someone so giddy about chocolate be a heartless killer? Again, I was assuming we had a killer in our midst.

We headed back into the pub. I awkwardly dropped the ice cream on the bar with a loud thump. The syrup toppled off the lid. Fortunately, the spout stayed closed.

"Who wants a brownie sundae?" I said, again mustering up my best cruise director enthusiasm.

"I'm in," Dave said.

"Oh no, I forget bowls." It hadn't been intentional, but it gave me the perfect opportunity to grab Henry's phone back.

"I'll get them," Rage said, and before I could stop him, he was already off his barstool and through the swinging door.

I sighed and worked on getting the lid off the ice cream.

Soon, Rage returned with bowls and spoons, and everyone began to make themselves a sundae. I sat beside Jack where he was positioned between myself and George, bellied up to the bar with everyone else. I held a bowl of ice cream for him to snack on.

"Sorry, Jackie boy," Dave said, as he squeezed a ridiculous amount of syrup onto his ice cream and brownie. "No chocolate for you."

"This would be a lot better if it was warm," Madeline said. She poked at the dessert she was determined to have.

"The pub would be a lot better if it was warm," Bryce grumbled, going over to the corner where his wool coat still hung over the back of a chair. He tugged it on. "Actually, everything would be a lot better if I wasn't even in this pub."

"That can be arranged," Dean muttered from beside me.

I rubbed his leg sympathetically. I was amazed that he hadn't actually confronted Bryce yet. He was probably figuring it would be best just to tell Justin about the assault and let him handle the situation. A barroom brawl was the last thing we needed tonight.

As if my current thoughts had conjured him, the door blew open, and Justin stumbled in. His body looked more like a snowman than a human, but his head was free of the crust of snow. Then I noticed a helmet in his hand.

I stood up immediately to greet him. Dean did as well.

"Hey there," I said. "I can't believe you made it."

Justin held up the helmet he was carrying. "Couple of the locals offered to let us use their snowmobiles for the night. Otherwise, I don't think I could have. I'm not even sure I could have made it tomorrow."

I tried not to groan. I didn't think I could handle being locked up in here with this group beyond tonight. Well, at least not a few of them.

"So, where is your dishwasher?"

"Well, nowhere near the actual dishwasher. So, he stuck to that pattern to the very end," Brandy piped in.

"He's in the stockroom," Dean said, ignoring Brandy's comment, and headed in that direction. Justin followed. So did I.

"I don't see how this can possibly be an accident. Someone hit him with some serious strength behind it," Justin said, after inspecting the wound on Henry's head for several minutes. "It definitely was not just a can falling off a shelf, that's for sure." He looked up at Dean and me both leaned in the doorway. "Do you have any thoughts on anyone who had a problem with him?"

"Honestly," I said, hoping I was not incriminating myself. "I think pretty much everyone here thought Henry was a creep."

"That is true," Dean said.

"Well, it's a big step from thinking someone is a creep and wanting him dead." Justin glanced down at the body again.

"Brett was talking to him quite a bit," I said. "Maybe when he sobers up you can ask him if he knows anything about Henry's personal life, or who might want him dead. They seemed to like each other. They hit it off instantly."

"That didn't last long though, though," Madeline said.

I jumped. What was she doing right behind us?

She giggled. "Sorry, didn't mean to scare you but I heard you talking about Henry and I wanted to tell the sheriff I heard him fighting with Brett."

"Really? Do you know what it was about?" Justin asked.

"I think Brett may have gotten the wrong impression about the nature of their friendship and Henry got angry with him."

Justin nodded. "But it was Henry who was angry?"

"I think they both were. They were shouting." Then she put her hands up in the air. "That's all I know." She went back toward the bar.

"That's interesting," Justin said.

"He was also a drug dealer," I added, getting a surprised look from both men.

"How do you know that?" Justin asked.

"Yes," Dean said, shifting toward me. "How do you know that?"

I made a pained face. "I may have found his phone."

"You went through his phone?" Justin said, clearly not pleased with my snooping. We'd had a couple issues in the past with me being too helpful. Well, I liked to call it being helpful. Justin might call it meddling. It was all a bit nitpicky, if you asked me.

"Did you find it before or after he was killed?" Justin studied me. I could tell he was trying to stay calm.

"Well." I knew that my explanation wasn't going to make either of the men particularly happy. "I found it on the floor. After he was struck and killed."

Justin rolled his eyes toward the ceiling. I had a feeling he was asking for divine province. "Sophie." Maybe it was working, because he sounded pretty calm. "I know that you know that is evidence tampering. What if there had been fingerprints or something that could've been usable on that phone?"

I winced again. "To be honest, I didn't actually think about it. I saw it laying there and I picked it up. But it does have a lot of interesting information on it. He has tons of texts. I'm sure there's something there that might hint at who could want him dead."

"Do you have the phone now?" Justin was still managing to sound calm.

I looked between the two men. "It's actually in the kitchen on Jimmy's desk. I'll go get it now." Without waiting for their response, I hurried to the kitchen.

I guess both Dean and Justin had valid points about me. I couldn't seem to control myself when it came to trying to find clues on my own. In retrospect, my New Year's resolution probably should have been to work on being less curious. I'd gone for the usual "eat better, work out more" resolution. But who was I kidding, even a twelve-hundred-calorie diet and an hour of cardio four times a week would be easier for me to stick to than not doing a little investigating every now and then. It was my thing. And I was pretty good at it.

When I stepped through the door, I saw that Janelle and Jimmy both still seemed to be sleeping.

I got my phone out and turned the flashlight on. I directed the light where I knew I'd left the phone. Then I slowly scanned the desk. Henry's phone was not there. I leaned down, looking around the floor. Maybe Janelle knocked it off the desk in her sleep. Other than a couple dropped pens and a rubber band, the floor was empty.

"Janelle," I said, softly. "Janelle?"

She shifted under the coat, then stretched. She squinted at me, then held her hand up in front of her face to block out the harsh light. I lowered it toward the desk.

"What?" she finally mumbled grumpily.

"Did you pick up a phone that was on the desk?"

She shook her head and closed her eyes again. "I can't find my phone."

That wasn't exactly the answer I was looking for, but I didn't think she had Henry's phone either. She curled into a tight ball on the chair and pulled Jimmy's coat up to cover her face.

I looked around the desk one last time, then headed back to the stockroom, the sinking feeling in my stomach growing heavier with each step.

"Got it?" Justin asked, holding out his large hand.

"Umm, the phone is gone."

TEN

JUSTIN HADN'T LOOKED in my direction since I told him about the phone, and I guess I couldn't blame him. On the upside, he had read Bryce his Miranda rights and was currently in the process of talking to Bryce about his assault on Dean. That seemed easier to address than trying to find out who killed Henry.

"You're saying that you did not hit Dean, knocking him unconscious?"

"No, I didn't," Bryce said, without a hint of guilt. He was more of a creep than Henry. Just a slightly more polished version.

Justin nodded slowly, skepticism clear on his face. "So, you're saying that everything your girlfriend told Sophie was a total lie?"

Bryce shot me a dirty look, then leaned forward in his chair. "You know how it is with women. She was mad at me about something else, so she just decided to cause some trouble. It was just a little misunderstanding that blew out of proportion. Isn't that right, baby?"

Lillian, who had been looking down at her hands, lifted her head to glare at him.

"No, *baby*. That isn't what happened. You told me that you thought Dean saw you leaving the barn, and so you picked up a fallen branch and hit him with it. You told me that you knocked him unconscious, but you didn't even stick around to see if that was the case. You left him out in a blizzard. And just in case you're planning to call me a liar again, I have all of that on my phone."

She looked at Justin. "My phone is locked in the safe, if you want it."

"Maybe where I could have locked Henry's phone," Dean murmured. "If you had told me about it."

I suspected he was more upset that I'd kept it a secret from him than the fact I'd had it at all. I gave him an appropriately remorseful look, while also making sure the others didn't hear him. I knew whoever took the phone was probably also Henry's murderer.

Behind us, we heard a loud clatter. Bryce had jumped up from his chair. It had fallen over in his anger. "You know what, Lillian, you really are a—"

"Okay, just sit down," Justin interrupted, standing.

Bryce glared at Lillian a moment longer. To Lillian's credit, she didn't move. She stayed in her chair, holding her ground.

Bryce left the knocked-over chair where it was and sank down into another one.

Justin approached him, cuffs in hand. "Put your hands out."

Bryce looked like he was going to argue, but then he did what he was told. Justin enclosed his wrist, then snapped the other cuff to the leg of the table.

"This is insane. Where am I going to go in a blizzard?"

Justin ignored his question. "If I were you, I'd just sit here quietly for now. And I wouldn't say another word to Lillian. It doesn't even matter if we have her recording, to be honest. We already know you were outside. That has been reported by several people here. We also know that someone hit Dean, as evident from his injury. And you even admitted that you had gone out to the barn to photograph Sienna's body. Do you really think that isn't enough evidence to arrest you for assault? The recording is just icing on the cake, my friend."

Bryce glared at him. "This is utterly insane."

Justin clearly had enough of this guy's attitude. "Maybe I should ask you a few questions about Henry. Since you like to bludgeon people in the head."

Bryce actually had the good grace to look worried. "Listen, I did not kill that guy in the stockroom."

Oliver leaned over to me and whispered, "What if he did kill Sienna?"

I frowned. "Why would he do that?"

"We've already seen he'll do anything for a new story. Who's to say he wouldn't kill to have the headline."

George, who was petting Jack and eavesdropping, leaned closer to add, "It could happen. Didn't you see that movie with that guy where he was a reporter or something, and he was actually doing all the bad things and then showing up first to get the breaking news."

I blinked. I had no idea what he was talking about.

"Oh yeah." Dave nodded. "That movie with Jake Gyllenhaal. What was that called?"

I still had no idea what they were talking about.

George, Oliver, and Dave continued to try to think of the name of the movie. This was when we really needed Google. But honestly, what difference did it make what it was called? The question at hand was Bryce.

Whatever the name of the movie, it did bring up a possible point. Maybe the murderer was already caught and handcuffed to a table. That possibility should make me feel better, but it didn't.

"Are you okay?" I asked Dean, who'd been quiet since telling Justin what he could recall of his attack.

He nodded. "I don't even know if I want to pursue any sort of legal action. Frankly, I'd be just as happy if Bryce Holden packed up and went back to L.A."

I had mixed feelings about that. He deserved to pay for his actions. There was no saying that he wouldn't do something like that again. But I also understood Dean just wanting everybody to go back home, so he could get back to his normal life. I laid my head on his shoulder. I had to admit I wanted the same thing.

"Sophie, Dean, I have to go," Justin said, from behind them. "Officer Young needs me to help transport a medical emergency. The ambulance can't make it in, so they need the snowmobile. I'll be back with Officer Young as soon as we can and we'll continue questioning everyone then."

I could tell he was reluctant to leave.

"We'll be fine," Dean assured him. He reached for my hand, reassuring me, too.

"What about Bryce? What if he has to go to the bathroom or something?" I asked quietly, glancing at Bryce. He leaned back in his chair, his free arm folded across his stomach. His other arm down beside the table, where his was attached. If he had been Grumpy Bryce before, he was now Livid Bryce now.

Lillian had moved to the bar, seated beside Madeline. Although Lillian didn't seem aware of any of us. She just stared down at the cup of tea that she held between her two hands.

Justin dug into his pocket, pulling out a small key. He handed it to Dean. After the phone situation, I knew he'd never put me in charge of it.

"If he has to go to the bathroom, make sure there are at least two of you with him. Take the big guy." Justin nodded toward Rage. Out of the corner of my eye, I saw Dave frown, crossing his arms over his chest, offended.

Oliver nodded agreement to Justin's suggestion. My friend clearly had no desire to play the role of prison guard.

"And just keep everyone together. I think everything will be fine." I could tell Justin wasn't totally sure of that. "I'll be back as soon as possible." He started across the room, then paused and came back. "Should I be concerned about that guy in the corner?"

Several of us glanced over at where Brett was still slumped.

"Oh no, he's fine. He just drank an incredible amount of whiskey. Aside from a killer stiff neck and the worst hangover probably known to man when he wakes up, he'll be okay."

"And let me state for the record right now, if by some sheer miracle, we wind up flying home tomorrow, I am not sitting beside him on the plane," Oliver stated loudly. "In fact, I want at least a three-row buffer, front and back."

Good call to make that clear now.

Justin nodded, looking as if he wasn't quite sure what to make of everything going on here. Without even commenting, he strode across the room, bundling up and grabbing his helmet. He stepped out into the blowing snow.

"Sheriff Justin is really a local hero," Oliver said with a sigh.

No sooner had the door closed, Bryce sat upright, his cuffs scraping in the table leg. "I hope you know that I'm going to sue everyone here."

"You're going to sue us?" Oliver said both stunned and amused. He rolled his eyes. "First of all, you're the one who assaulted a person. And second of all, you're also the one who created and sold a story that was ridiculous." Oliver considered that for a moment. "Well, most of the story for *Hollywood Has Beens* might have been somewhat accurate. But you can't possibly think that you were going to get away with taking pictures of some poor dead woman for a buck?"

"It's news," Bryce stated. "The public wants and deserves the facts."

Umm, we didn't exactly have many facts yet, but I didn't bother to say that. I knew that was just his excuse to defend indefensible behavior anyway. "We should sue you for impersonating a legitimate reporter," I said, thoroughly disgusted with Bryce. "As for assaulting Dean, the sheriff might press assault charges, you know."

Rage hopped up from his stool, gripping the edge of the bar to steady himself. Uh-oh, it looked like all the wine he'd been drinking this evening had finally gotten to him. We might have to rethink who was on prison guard duties. And possibly, when to cut off our patrons.

"You photographed a dead woman," he growled, most of his

words said without slurring. He pointed a finger at Bryce. "You are nothing but a lowlife scumbag."

Bryce looked totally unaffected by the insult. I'm sure he'd heard it often enough. "Oh, are you having guilt or something?"

"What are you even talking about?" Madeline said, scowling at the shady celebrity reporter.

Before Bryce could say something hateful and offensive in response to her, Rage said, "I do have guilt. A lot of guilt."

Everybody's attention turned to him. Guilt? Was he about to admit that he knew something about Sienna's death?

He wiped a hand over his face as if trying to clear away his thoughts. "I cannot believe she's gone."

He sounded totally defeated and heartbroken.

Madeline touched his arm. "None of us can, baby."

Rage shook off her touch and stepped away from her. He turned to face her. "I feel guilty about you, too. You were right about me and Sienna. She was flirting with me this whole week. She definitely was coming on to me, and I lied to you when I said it was nothing. I lied when I said I had no feelings for Sienna."

Oh no.

Madeline looked around at everyone, embarrassed. I could also see anger simmering in her big, brown eyes. "Rage, we don't have to talk about this right now."

"I don't think it matters much," George said, pragmatically. "I'm pretty sure just about everyone here saw you two arguing at some point."

"Shut up, you weird old drunk," Madeline said to him from down the bar.

I blinked at the venom in her voice.

George straightened his John Deere hat, looking surprisingly unaffected by her comment. "I just call it like I see it, toots."

"It's true," Rage said. "We haven't been working out, Mads. I really tried on this trip. Honestly, I did. But being around Sienna made me realize how much I missed her."

"Missed her?" Oliver shook his head confused. "I didn't even know you two knew each other before the casting for *Hayley and Jake*."

Rage turned to Oliver. "Sienna and I dated for about six months about a year ago. We were pretty serious, but then Sienna got cold feet and broke things off."

Oliver nodded. "Sienna always had commitment issues. It was because of her mom's endless circle of bad relationships."

"Yes, that's why I didn't take her seriously when she told me she wanted to work things out. I thought she was just jealous about me being with Mads."

"She was," Madeline said, leaning forward to touch him again.

I felt bad for Madeline. I could totally understand why she didn't want to hear this, much less in front of all of us.

Again, Rage shifted away. "No, she was being honest. And I'd made up my mind to end things with you once we got home. I couldn't do it here. You didn't deserve that."

It could be argued that she didn't deserve it this way either. This was painful. And it wasn't a particularly good idea to air all their drama in front of Bryce. He was probably mentally writing his next scandal piece as they spoke.

"Maybe we should let you two talk about this alone," I said. Of course, there wasn't really much of anywhere for us to go. "Maybe you two could talk in the restroom."

Dean frowned. "We're supposed to stay together."

"Do you really want to be a part of this mess?" I whispered.

"I'm sorry, Madeline. I never wanted to hurt you. But I had to give Sienna another chance. She needed me."

Madeline started crying. "I need you."

Dean made a face that said he could see my point about being stuck in the middle of this ugly breakup.

Brandy made a big show of gathering up dirty glasses and putting them in a gray bus bucket. She headed to the kitchen.

"Wait, buddy system," Dave called, following her.

I knew he wanted to get away from the uncomfortable scene just like Brandy. They disappeared into the kitchen. Lillian had even opted to leave the bar and sit at the opposite end of the table where Bryce was cuffed. Even Jack had decided to make a bed for himself on the other side of the pub, his eyes closed and his ears occasionally twitching when Madeline wailed.

"I need to use the john," George said, not waiting for his buddy. He strode toward the restrooms, giving the still arguing Madeline and Rage a wide berth.

"I need to go too," Bryce announced.

"Everyone thinks I'm nothing but a stupid redhead," Madeline shouted at Rage, tears streaming down her face. "But I have plans. And you are ruining them."

Rage answered, but I couldn't hear what he was saying over Madeline's sobs.

"I have to go to the restroom," Bryce insisted again. He tugged at his restraint. I was suddenly glad the old tables weighed a ton.

Dean stood, grabbing the handcuff key of the bar. I rose, too. Dean was going to need backup. Plus, I didn't want to stay behind with the reality-show-worthy breakup going on just a few feet from the bar.

"It's okay," Dean said. "George is in there, if I need help."

I gave him a "thanks for nothing" look, but nodded. On second thought, I didn't want to be in the men's room with George and Bryce either.

Dean unlocked Bryce and then made him hold out his hands so he could snap the open cuff onto Bryce's freed wrist.

"This is all ridiculous," Bryce muttered as they walked past me.

"Almost as ridiculous as bashing someone on the head and leaving him in the snow?" I said back. Bryce sneered at me, but kept walking with Dean.

"I have to go to the bathroom, too," Lillian said, standing. "Will you go with me?"

I glanced around, realizing other than the still fighting couple, my llama, and unconscious Brett, we were the only ones left in the pub area.

"Yeah, I'll go with you." It seemed even more awkward listening to Madeline and Rage's fight with everyone else gone.

We both headed to the ladies' room. Once inside, both Lillian and I let out a sigh of relief.

"Man, that was seriously uncomfortable." Lillian leaned on the door as if gathering herself.

"This has been the weirdest day of my life," I admitted, and frankly, I'd had some weird times here in Friendship Harbor already.

"Agreed." Lillian headed to one of the bathroom stalls.

I went to the sinks, leaning on the Formica counter and peering into the mirror. My hair was snarled and staticky, and my face was completely devoid of makeup. I looked as if I'd been through some crap. Which I had.

"I guess I should thank you for handling your breakup much less dramatically." As soon as the words left my lips, I regretted them. To be honest, I had no idea if Lillian and Bryce were actually broken up. Although it seemed unlikely given the Lillian had turned Bryce into the sheriff that they were going to work things out.

But to my relief, she laughed. "I know exactly where Rage was coming from. I fully intended to break up with Bryce and quit my job as soon as I got back to L.A. I was just trying to get through this assignment. But criminal behavior is where I draw the line on keeping things status quo."

"Well, thank you," I said sincerely as I tried to calm my wild hair. "I think what you did was really brave. Both Dean and I appreciate it."

"I'm just glad it's over, and I did what had to be done." She was silent for a moment, then she added, "Maybe we should bring Madeline some tissues or something. And maybe a wet cloth. That might help calm her down. Being angry *and* red and puffy just makes everything that much worse."

I nodded even though I knew Lillian couldn't see me. That was a good idea. Nothing added insult to injury than looking like a total wreck after a meltdown. I pulled several paper towels out of the dispenser and started to wet them. Then my hands stopped as a realization hit me.

Red puffy eyes. The empty bottle of eye drops. Henry's weird, cryptic text about using eye drops.

I needed to retrieve that bottle Jack had found. It could possibly be evidence. In fact, I was willing to bet it was. I wasn't sure exactly how the eye drops had been used. But I was willing to bet if I could figure out who owned the bag that the eye drops had fallen out of, I could pinpoint who killed Henry. And maybe even Sienna.

"Lillian, are you okay in here by yourself for a second? I'm going to run to the kitchen to get a rag to wet down for Madeline."

"Yeah, I'm fine. I'm actually enjoying the peace."

I got that.

Carefully opening the door, I peeked out. The pub was empty except for Jack and Brett, sleeping in their prospective corners. Dean, Bryce, and George must still be in the men's room.

And I had no idea where Madeline and Rage had gone.

That was a little concerning, but right now, I had to take the opportunity to sneak into the office while I had it. Cell phone out and flashlight on, I quickly left the bathroom and headed through the stockroom into the office.

The office was empty, and for a brief moment, I wondered again where Madeline and Rage could have gone. Not far. Not with the storm still blowing full force. I turned my attention to the black nylon carry-on bag. I knew when I'd thrown the bottle back into the bag that I hadn't bothered with the zipper. So, that meant someone had to have been back here. Great, I hoped the eye drop bottle was still in there.

Slowly I unzipped it, the opening of the nylon teeth sounding so loud in the dark, silent room. I paused once, listening for any signs of someone approaching. Not a sound. Once the bag was open, I shined the light inside.

I spotted the eye drop bottle right away. I shoved it in the front pocket of my sweatpants. The likelihood that there would be any fingerprints were nil, but if I could figure out who the bag belonged to, then I would know who owned the bottle.

I shined the light back into the bag, looking for something that would indicate who it belonged to. I remembered there was a wallet that I'd thrown back into the bag, but that was missing now, too.

Darn it.

Then something else caught my eye. Henry's phone.

ELEVEN

I SWIPED the screen and it lit up.

I opened the texts again, rereading the one about the eye drops. *Eye drops, huh? Sneaky, sneaky.*

Someone had done something with eye drops. But what and who?

I stared at the initial code. SRH. Only Sienna and I were they ones here whose names started with an S. And the rest of the letters didn't match our names at all.

I hesitated a moment longer, then decided to go for it. I hit the button to call SRH. I could hear it ringing. Only I realized it wasn't just ringing on the other end of Henry's phone. I could hear it ringing in reality. Somewhere in the building with me. Unnerved, but triumphant that my hunch was correct, I tried to ascertain where the sound was coming from.

Wait a minute. It was getting closer. The phone went to voicemail.

Whoever it belonged to didn't have a personalized greeting. It was just the robot voice telling me to leave a message. I ended the call and dialed it again, knowing if the sound was getting closer, someone in the building had it in their possession. They were SRH.

The door to the office opened and I whipped around, fearful of having been busted with Henry's phone. It was Madeline, her phone to her ear. "Hello?" she said.

Her greeting echoed in my own ear. I swallowed hard.

"Hello?" she repeated. "Who is this?" Then she looked me straight in the eye, all her childlike vapidity gone. Her expression looked cold and maniacal. "Henry, is that you? Calling from the dead?" She gave a giggle.

The sound made goose bumps hurtle up the length of my spine. I just stood there.

"I can hear you breathing into the phone, Sophie," she said. "I know you're on Henry's phone and I know you know. I just wish you weren't so darned nosy." She ended the call and shoved her phone in her pocket. For having been caught, she looked mostly unconcerned.

"I don't know what you're talking about," I said.

"It's not what you're thinking. It was actually an accident. Sienna, I mean. I was friends with Sienna. I never meant for anything to happen to her."

I dropped my arm holding the phone and eyed Madeline. She looked less frightening now, but I was very aware of the fact that she was between me and the door.

"I could have sworn you said that was Janelle's phone, which I found kind of funny. Because..." She reached into her pocket and pulled out another phone. Her lips made an O of faux surprise as she held it up. "I have Janelle's phone."

I frowned. "Why do you have Janelle's phone?"

"I thought it would be smarter to text Henry on her phone. He was a real money-grubbing hustler, Sophie. Harassing me. He got Brett to give him my number, can you believe that? You need to screen your staff better."

"Why was he harassing you?"

The weird look on her face was replaced by a pleading expression. "I just wanted Sienna to get a little sick, maybe puke a few times. She couldn't be trying to steal my man if her head's in a toilet, you know what I mean? I figured once we got home, I could work on securing my relationship with Rage. Maybe get pregnant or something, I don't know, I was working on that."

Bonkers alert. Nothing like dragging an innocent infant into a disastrous relationship on purpose. Not to mention that was manipulating the heck out of Rage. "So you put the eye drops in Sienna's drink and then encouraged the idea that she was using drugs again?"

"It sounds so bad when you say it like that," Madeline said, her lip pulling down in a pout. "I thought she would throw up and just look gross and that would be the end of it. I mean, maybe she just fell down in the snow and died from exposure. It's not like we really know. It might not even be my fault."

With every word, she perked up. It was like she was convincing herself she wasn't responsible. "She did have a drug problem at one time," she added. "Maybe she was high and drinking wine and fell down in the snow."

Or unwittingly drank an entire bottle of eye drops. I wasn't totally sure that could kill her either, but it couldn't have done her any good. I suddenly recalled the full glass of wine that Madeline had knocked over earlier. That must have been the wine for Sienna. And it must have had eye drops in it, too. I guess I could give Madeline props for not letting anyone else drink it. Not huge props but some.

"Where did Henry fit into this?" I asked. "He wasn't supplying Sienna with drugs, was he?"

"I have no idea. He could have been. If he was a drug dealer and she was a former user, how do we know the truth? Maybe she was his customer all week long."

Madeline was definitely delusional. The police would know the truth as soon as a toxicology report was run at Sienna's autopsy. But I needed Madeline relaxed and talking, so I let her have her little fantasy. "Then why kill Henry?"

It had to have been her. No one else would have the motive. Sure, Henry had possessed a notoriously creepy smile, but he barely knew anyone who worked at Steamy's and had almost zero contact with the California guests. There would be no reason for anyone to want him dead except for Madeline, who had received texts from him making it obvious he had seen what she had done.

His text had spelled it out very clearly.

But now I wanted her to say it out loud so I could tell Justin she had confessed.

Still gripping Henry's phone, I was prepared to press 911 if need be, though I wasn't sure who would respond to my call. The storm was still raging outside.

"He didn't give me a choice," Madeline said.

It was when she lifted her hand that I realized she was holding a gummy worm. She bit the end off of it viciously, as if she wasn't even aware she was doing it, but stress eating.

It sent another chill up my spine.

"He was being super mean to me," she added. "He was going to make it seem like it was all my fault about Sienna. He was going to ruin my career, my relationship with Rage, and get me in trouble. He wouldn't even listen when I tried to explain it was an accident. He wanted me to pay him to stay quiet." She bit the worm again. "He just wouldn't stop and I got so mad and I thought everyone would think Brett did it. I figured if I said they were arguing, you would think it was him. He's stronger than me. And he was so drunk, he probably wouldn't know if he'd done it or not."

"Brett was a good person to pin it on," I said. "Kudos on that one, Madeline."

She gave me a sweet smile. "Thank you. I'm not as dumb as everyone thinks."

But much, much crazier.

"You won't tell, will you, Soph?" She gave me a pleading look.

Definitely bonkers. "Madeline, two people are dead because of you." I almost told her that my first order of business was going to be to tell the sheriff everything, but then I realized that if she had the strength to nail Henry in the noodle with stewed toma-toes, she was stronger than she looked. She was still blocking my exit.

Why was no one questioning how long I had been gone? Lillian thought I was in the kitchen. And everyone in the kitchen had no idea where I was. I cursed myself mentally for not telling Lillian what I was really doing. But I had been trying to be sneaky.

Great job, Soph.

No one would have any reason to come into the office unless they thought I was in jeopardy.

"Where is Rage?" I asked, hoping maybe he knew she'd come in here.

"He's sleeping. He had too much to drink." She giggled.

Oh sweet mother, what had she done to Rage? And how many murders constituted a serial killer?

"So, this will be our little secret, right?" Madeline said, searching my face. "We've always been such good friends."

I wasn't sure how good of friends we could have been since I clearly never knew her. Not really.

But I nodded and managed a smile. "Sure. We can keep this a secret."

I took a step back while slipping Henry's phone into my pocket. If I could make a run for the hallway, I could go out my front door and across the porch to the pub. Or I could just scream and hope someone came running.

Madeline took a step forward too. She pulled another gummy worm from her pocket and bit into it as if it was her enemy. "You know, Soph, you never were a very good actress."

She darted forward and picked up a large, heavy-duty-style hole punch from Dean's desk. The circles of paper from making holes scattered all over the floor like confetti.

Surprise. I was about to get attacked.

I spun toward the hallway, jerking open the door. I tried to close the door behind me. There was a deadbolt, if I could get it closed. But she was already there, her arm and the hole punch waving toward me. I tried to shove the door closed and hold on to my phone for the light.

She yelped as I pushed the door harder, but she didn't retreat. I was going to have to let the door go and just run for it. I gave the door one more hard shove, hoping it might injure her enough to slow her down. Then I ran. I tripped over the blanket I had put down for Jack but managed to keep my footing.

I reached my front door, but I could tell from the light bouncing off the walls around me that she was close behind. Fortunately, the lock unlatched easily, although I kept my head down, expecting any minute that the hole punch would bash me on the head. Throwing open the door, I raced outside only to be greeted by knee-high snow. Even the porch was covered with the heavy white stuff. The wind and the pelting snow disoriented me for a moment, but then I gathered myself and prepared to run it in the direction of the pub. But I never made a step before I was full-on body checked. We both fell onto the porch, sinking in the drift. Neither of us moved for a split second, but then I managed to scramble to my feet. I started wading through the snow, but again she caught me. I pulled away, only to slip and roll down the steps to my front yard.

Madeline half climbed/half slid down behind me. She launched herself onto me and we both sank deep into the snow. I couldn't even see anything other than her looming over me.

She grabbed my neck, her fingers digging into my skin. I tried to claw at them, but she was strong. But there was no way in the world I was dying half buried in the snow at the hands of a crazy, washed-up, child actor.

I braced my hands on either side of me, and with a banshee cry, I flipped her over. She sank deep into the snow and I scrambled to straddle her. I tried to use my weight to subdue her, but she was still insanely strong and she pushed me off. I tried to crab-crawl backwards away from her, but the snow created a wall behind me and my hands and feet kept sinking. She lunged forward again. Again, I was pinned.

"Madeline," I said, breathless. "You don't need to do this. It's over anyway. It's over."

She pulled back, still sitting on my legs. I couldn't see her features in the dark and I had no idea where either of our phones were. I dug into my sweatpants pocket. Somehow, I still had Henry's phone. I tried several times to turn on the flashlight. My fingers were numb and wet. The phone wouldn't react. Finally, the screen unlocked and the homescreen appeared. I tapped the flashlight app and then levered myself up on one arm, shining the light at her.

Madeline's face was covered with tangled red hair and clumps of snow. Her shoulders shook.

"I just wanted my career back. I wanted to be famous again. Really famous. Not some has-been. I wanted a hit show. To be half of a perfect Hollywood dream couple. This was my second chance. This was my second chance."

Was all this really that simple? She'd seen her second change being destroyed and she'd lost her mind. I actually believed it was.

Just then, I heard the rev of engines in the distance, then I saw headlights reflecting off of the falling snow and the drifts all around us.

"Everything okay?" A voice yelled out from the vehicle.

I almost collapsed back into the snow. I knew that was the sheriff's voice. But with Madeline calmer and Justin here, the danger was diminished and I realized something— I seriously hated the cold and snow.

"I'm okay," I managed to yell.

"Get off of her," I heard Justin's voice over the wind. "Stand up and back away from her."

To my surprise, Madeline did what he said, struggling to her feet, her hands held limply in the air. She said nothing as Officer Young appeared and placed handcuffs on her. She didn't even look remotely like the sweet, ditzy redhead I'd know for years. She looked like the insane villain from a Lifetime movie.

If she wanted to be famous, this was going to do it. A murder trial of a former child actor would get lots of airtime.

Justin helped me to my feet. "Are you okay?"

I nodded. "She killed Sienna and Henry. Maybe Rage."

It was hard to believe the meek woman being led back to the pub was a killer. But she played her final role to a tee. But I guess even Madeline knew when it was time to admit this was the finale.

TWELVE

"ARE YOU OKAY, RAGE?"

Now, Madeline's sweet voice only sounded creepy to me now. I could only imagine how it sounded to Rage as he sat at the bar as far away from her as he could. He refused to look at her, instead focusing on the bar top, holding a bag of peas to his head.

"Keep quiet," Officer Young said to Madeline, who was now cuffed to a table just like Bryce. This whole situation was so surreal.

"He's my boyfriend," Madeline snapped her indignantly. "And he's hurt."

Officer Young raised an eyebrow at her comment. I'm pretty sure I did, too. Did Madeline honestly not recall how Rage got hurt and that she was the one who did it? A wine bottle over the head could have killed him, too. Or did she still just expect that she would be forgiven. She brought cray cray to a whole new level.

Justin came over to me. I could tell by the grim set of his mouth, he wasn't pleased with me. I can't say I was surprised.

"Can you tell me exactly what happened? For my report?"

"Yes. Of course." I glanced at Dean, but he didn't seem much more pleased with me than Justin. Fantastic.

Justin pointed to a table that was in the corner away from the two prisoners. I gathered the blanket I had wrapped around me, which wasn't doing much to warm me up. My clothes were damp, and I couldn't stop shivering. I knew it was a combination of cold and adrenaline. I managed to stand and lead the way to the table he indicated.

We both sat down, and Justin pulled out a small pad of paper from inside his coat. But before he asked me any questions, he stared at me.

"Sophie, I know you think you are helping. But all you are going to do is get yourself really hurt or worse."

As far as reprimands went, this was a pretty gentle one. And I knew he was right.

"I know. If it's any consultation, I didn't think this was going to go the way it did. I was just trying to make sure I rescued possible evidence before it went missing. I didn't expect to be snow wrestling."

I reached under my blanket and fumbled to get the bottle and phone out of my damp pockets. I placed them on the table, hoping the phone still worked after getting wet from the snow.

He took both. He tapped the screen and it illuminated. I had a feeling that my phone, lost outside somewhere, probably hadn't fared as well.

He set both items aside and returned to the inner pocket of his jacket and pulled out a pen.

I told him what Madeline had said to me and everything that transpired, while Justin made notes. When I was done, Justin sighed and glanced back to Madeline.

"What will happen to her?" I asked, still torn between feeling sympathy for the Madeline I thought I knew and the one I'd seen tonight. That one that was totally off her rocker.

"Officer Young is going to stay with both Madeline and Bryce until we can move them to the jail and then we will go from there."

I nodded, immediately feeling better about having law enforcement here to watch them.

"I would suggest everyone else go up to your place. I think it's best to be away from these two."

I agreed with him. From behind us, there was a low groan.

Brett sat up, blinking and rubbing his head. "What's going on," he grumbled. He squinted into the shadowy candlelight, taking in the scene in front of him. Rage with his bag of peas. Bryce and Madeline handcuffed to tables. Two officers, looking stressed and exhausted. And the rest of us in various states of shock.

"I feel like I missed something," he finally said. No one bothered to answer him. It was too long a story to tell anyway. He made an alarmed face, clapped a hand over his mouth, and scrambled to his feet. With a mad dash to the men's room, he burst through the door, which was followed by the slam of the stall door and a retching sound.

"I'm not following the buddy system with this one," Oliver stated. No one else moved either. We probably didn't need the buddy system anymore anyway.

Justin stood up. "Okay everyone. I think you should all head up to Sophie's place. Officer Young and I have everything under control here."

"What about Jack?" Dave asked.

"I'll stay with him," George said. He left his barstool and settled on the floor beside where Jack snoozed. Jack's ear twitched, but he didn't lift his head from where it rested on a chair like it was a pillow. George propped his back against the wall and crossed his arm over his chest. As far as resting places went, it didn't look too comfortable. But I did appreciate his willingness to watch my pet.

I got a pillow and blanket from the pile Rage had brought in earlier and carried them over to George.

"Thank you," I said sincerely.

George nodded. "Your llama is better company than lots of people." He arranged the pillow between his head and the wall and draped the blanket over him.

"Let's get everyone upstairs and find them places to sleep,"

Dean said, appearing beside me. He put an arm around my back, and I sank against him. I was exhausted.

"Better yet, why don't you head up and I'll get everyone settled," he said, giving me a concerned squeeze.

"That sounds great." I was freezing and sore and tired.

"You can't just leave me here," Madeline said pitifully. She still didn't seem to understand the huge amount of trouble she was in. "I'm cold and tired. Why can't I go up too?"

Bryce glared at her. I'm not sure I'd want to listen to her whining all night either.

"I'll stay with you," Rage said.

"Are you sure, man?" Oliver asked him quietly.

Rage nodded. "I can't leave her like this. I owe her that much."

Oliver looked unconvinced. I was in Oliver's camp. I didn't think Rage should feel as guilty as he did. Madeline kind of lost the right to play the injured ex when she started knocking off people.

Brandy gathered up all the rest of the extra bedding. "I'll go up with you."

"We'll be right behind you," Dean said. "I'll help Brett get upstairs."

"Yeah, I will too," Oliver said. I wasn't sure if that was for my benefit or just to get away from Madeline and Bryce. I didn't care as long as I could get into dry clothes and my bed.

Once we got upstairs and we'd lit some candles, Brandy immediately started making up the couch in the living room. "Dave and I can crash in here. And I'll figure out where the others will crash. You can go up to your room and change."

"Are you sure?" I asked.

She nodded. "Are you okay going up stairs alone?"

"I'm a little shaken up, but I feel better knowing Officer Young will be here."

"Me too," Brandy admitted. "I'm also glad that we'll be up here and there are a lot of us."

That was true. It did feel safer being in my own space and

away from all the crazy. I picked up a candle. "Just call if you need anything."

Brandy nodded. "It will be fine."

I headed upstairs. After gathering a pair of fleece pajamas and a thick robe that had belonged to my Grammy, I went into the bathroom and drew a bath, very pleased that the water was still warm. By candlelight, I climbed in the tub to soak my chilled, aching body. What a night.

WHEN I CAME out of the bathroom, a half an hour later, I started to find Dean sitting on my bed.

"Sorry, I didn't mean to scare you. I just wanted to be sure you were alright," he said.

I nodded, shoving my hands in the robe pockets. "I feel much better." And I was pleased to see him. This was the first time he'd ever even been in my room. He'd lived in the guest house, and then moved in with me once we decided to make the guesthouse into a vacation rental to help make extra money during the slow season for the pub. Now, he lived across town, because we both had agreed working together, living together and dating was a lot for a brand new relationship.

But I couldn't deny I was glad he was here tonight.

"Is everyone settled?" The house was quiet.

"Yeah. Oliver, Lillian and Janelle are in the guestrooms. Brett is on the guest bathroom floor, hating life. Brandy and Dave are in the living room. And Rage is still staying with Madeline."

"Where is Jimmy?"

"In his kitchen," Dean smiled lopsidedly.

"Or course. He loves that kitchen."

"He really does."

I sat down on my bed beside him. "And you are here."

"I can sleep in the living room too," he said. "I just wanted to make sure you are okay."

"I am."

Dean nodded and started to push up from my bed. I reached for his hand to stop him. "But I'd like you to stay."

Dean's eyes met mine, his gaze probing. "Soph, I don't—"

"No, I don't mean like that." The timing was definitely not right for *that*. "I just would feel better having you here."

His gaze roamed my face. "If you're sure."

"I am."

He rose and pulled back the covers so I could crawl under them, then he went around the other side of the bed and did the same. We laid there, neither of us speaking.

"Dean, can I ask you something?" I finally said.

"Sure."

"Are we dating?"

He turned his head, giving me a confused look. "Umm, yes. I thought that was pretty clear."

"I mean like exclusively." I felt awkward asking, but we never really discussed what we were doing exactly.

He smiled. "I'd like that. Why, do you have other plans?"

"No," I said a little too quickly. "No, I have no other plans. I'd like to be exclusive."

Dean rolled over to kiss me sweetly. "I really like you, Soph. Even though your uncanny ability to get yourself into dangerous positions does make me a little crazy."

My heart pitter-pattered merrily. "I really like you, too, Dean. And I can try to do better about the danger prone thing."

He pulled me closer and I rested my head on his chest.

"Maybe we could start by keeping our dates murder-free," he said.

"Absolutely." Despite the awful events of the day, I felt my body relax. Soon, I was drifting off to sleep, safe and warm, curled against Dean. It was a wonderful ending to a less than wonderful day.

"SO ARE YOU, like, crazy happy to be back in L.A.?" I asked

Oliver as I settled back on my sofa with a glass of pinot noir. I could see on my laptop screen that my friend was sitting out on his apartment balcony, palm trees waving in the breeze behind him.

"I'm glad to be out of that wild Maine weather. But eh." He shrugged.

I frowned. We hadn't talked since he got back to California, other than a few texts. It had been at least two weeks. This was a new, and not good, record for us. But I guess we all needed time to recover. "What's going on? Are you okay?"

He sighed, then nodded. "Well, the *Hayley and Jake* reboot is officially dead." He grimaced. "That probably wasn't the best phrasing."

I winced slightly in agreement. "I'm sorry."

"It wasn't exactly a surprise."

"What about your Lifetime audition?"

"I did get a part." He didn't look thrilled.

"That's good, right?"

"I'm dental patient number three. I didn't even get dental patient one or two. And I have no lines."

"I'm sorry."

"The worst part is that Brett auditioned for another LIfetime movie and got a major part. He's the villain. A crazy stalker ex-husband."

"That's not exactly a stretch for him though."

He rolled his eyes, but agreed."True."

"How is Rage?"

Oliver took a sip of his wine, then said, "He's actually taking some time off from acting. He's working as a personal trainer."

I could see that. "Have you heard anything about Madeline?" I'd asked Justin, but he wasn't sharing much with me. I understood why, even though Madeline had been a friend.

"Well, I did find out that Sienna did die from an overdose of eye drops. I had no idea that could even happen."

I didn't either. But I wasn't totally surprised.

"But Madeline's parents apparently hired a big-time lawyer

and they got the court to agree to her getting a psychiatric evaluation. Last I heard, she was in an institution." Oliver shook his head and took a sip of wine.

"I'm not surprised. I think she had a total mental break."

Oliver took another swallow of his wine. "In a big way. Soph, I think I'm sort of over Hollywood. I think you made a good choice walking away. I keep thinking about how the need to be famous, the need to get attention, was the thing that pushed Mads over the edge. It's not good. You were so wise to get out of here."

I couldn't disagree—at least for myself. Even with the snow and the cold and the less than glamorous job as a pub owner, I didn't miss the whole competitive and fake nature of fame. Especially in Hollywood.

"But get this," Oliver said, perking up. "That assistant of Bryce Holden..."

"Lillian."

He nodded, his expression animated and back to his old self for the first time since we started talking. "Yeah, Lillian. She's got her own show. Hollywood This Week. It's actually pretty good. Like legit interviews and news. No trashy gossip."

"You like the trashy gossip,"

"I do," he admitted. "Unless it involves me or my friends. By the way, you are not a has-been. You are a doing-something-different. And I personally think showing a llama is very cool."

I gave him a touched smile. "Thank you."

"Although can you please, please promise me your new life won't involve quite so much murder?"

I sighed. "I definitely want that, too. In fact, I've decided to focus on romance."

Oliver straightened up and moved closer to his camera. "Do tell. I want all the Dean deets."

I laughed at his eagerness. "Well, we have been on some pretty amazing dates."

He groaned, disappointed. "Lame deets, Soph."

"I can tell you that he's pretty special."

He rolled his eyes. "Also lame. But also adorbs. And I don't blame you for focusing on romance with a hunk like him. I'm openly jealous."

"You'll find your Mr. Right," I assured him. "In fact, I've decided that will be my focus. Finding perfect matches for my friends."

"Okay, that might be scarier than murder. You're going to be a matchmaker?"

"Yeah," I said, refusing to be dissuaded by the skepticism in his voice. "I'm planning to do a Bachelor/Bachelorette auction. It will be a great fundraiser of the pub and an even better way to get my single friends mingling."

Oliver still looked unconvinced.

"You know you want to come be a part of it."

"Only if you and Dean do it, too."

I hadn't considered that, but shrugged. "Why would we do that? We're dating."

"Okay, my bestie, I have to go. I actually booked an appointment with Rage. I need to get buffed up."

I suspected Oliver was really going to workout with Rage just to support him.

"Okay." I toasted him with my wine. "I'm going to cuddle under my blanket, drink my wine, and probably watch a Hallmark movie."

"Maybe I should audition for one of those?" He considered the idea for a moment, then shook his head. "Nah, I'm too snarky for them."

"Agreed."

"Okay, love you, Soph."

"Love you, too."

I disconnected my laptop from the call and leaned back on my sofa, feeling better to actually chat with Oliver. Then my thoughts moved on to my new plan. A bachelor/bachelorette auction. It was a good idea.

After all, matchmaking—what could go wrong with that?

ABOUT THE AUTHORS

USA Today and New York Times Bestselling author Erin McCarthy sold her first book in 2002 and has since written over eighty novels in teen fiction, romance, and mysteries. Erin has a special weakness for high-heeled boots, Frank Sinatra, and martinis. She lives with her husband and their blended family of kids and rescue pets.

Connect with Erin:
www.erinmccarthymysteries.com

Kathy Love is a USA Today best selling author of over twenty-five books. She has written in several genres, including contemporary and paranormal romance and horror. Kathy loves all things groovy and retro, especially The Beatles, flower power and disco balls. But she also loves ghost stories, Halloween and New Orleans. What can she say, she's eclectic. Kathy grew up in Maine but now lives in Maryland with her family, three rescue mutts and four rescue cats. It's a full house!

Made in the USA
Monee, IL
10 July 2021